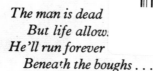

The man is dead
But life allow.
He'll run forever
Beneath the boughs . . .

The running dead man is part of the Legend of the Golden Key which, since 1798, has haunted the imagination of successive generations.

One beautiful summer day, with swallows skimming over the river and the willow trees on the river in full midsummer splendour, five young hopefuls decide to solve the mystery of the Golden Key.

Old Daddy Armstrong tells them the story behind the legend, a tale as old as time, of a beautiful young girl who defies her miserly father and his promise of a fortune in gold and chooses instead to wed her penniless lover.

The young lovers disappear, but what of the fortune. . .?

Tapser and his friends start their quest at the castle, once the home of the miserly father of the legend. There are strange happenings in the grounds, unexplained lights are seen from the fairy fort on Wariff Hill, mysterious sounds are heard late at night in the castle.

Can they solve the riddle? Will the treasure be found. . .?

TOM McCAUGHREN is Security Correspondent at RTE, the national television station. His spare-time activity is writing, particularly children's books.

The Legend of the Golden Key, now published in full as originally written, captures the sounds and scents of midsummer. As in all Tom McCaughren's books, the background of flora and fauna is marvellously drawn, and there is a haunting evocation of all one's childhood fantasies in the walk through sinister woods at night.

'The maximum amount of enjoyment, with a discreet educational element skilfully woven into the story. . .'   EVENING PRESS

Tom McCaughren

The Legend of the Golden Key

Illustrated by Terry Myler

THE CHILDREN'S PRESS

To my daughters –
Michelle, Amanda, Samantha and Simone

First published 1988 by
The Children's Press
45 Palmerston Road, Dublin 6

Paperback edition 1989
Reprinted 1991, 1993

Abridged edition published 1983 by
The Children's Press

ISBN 0 937962 36 0

Typesetting by Computertype Ltd., Dublin
Printed by Colour Books Limited

CONTENTS

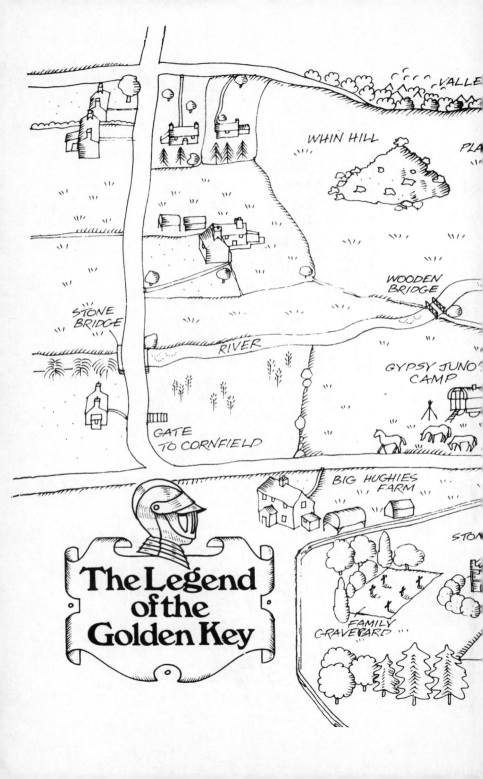

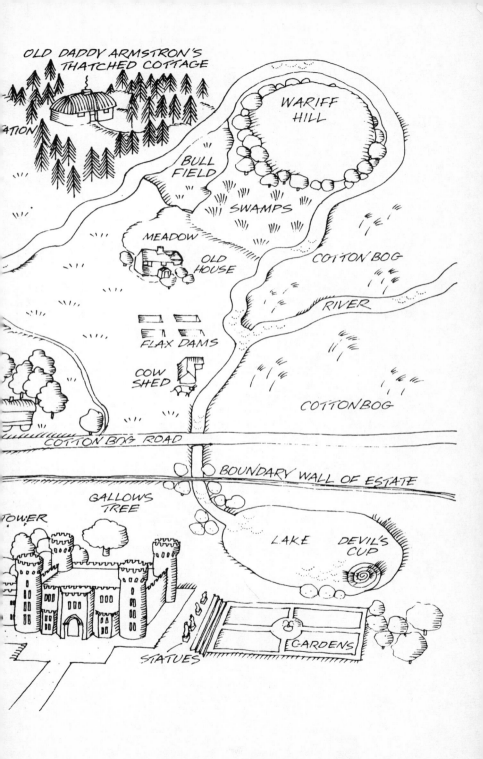

INTRODUCTION

When *The Legend of the Golden Key* was first published in 1983, it was shortened so as to make a compact paperback. Over the years it has proved to be one of the most popular books I have written for young people, and this year The Children's Press and I felt we owed it to our readers to publish the story in its entirety as originally written. It was the original version that my eldest daughter, Michelle, read and she still recalls it as one of the happiest memories of her childhood.

In the course of visits to schools, libraries and book fairs in both parts of Ireland, many young people have asked me if the legend is true. The answer is, 'Not exactly!' However, many aspects of it are based on fact, and some of the settings are real.

While the story could just as easily have taken place in County Wexford or any other county in Ireland, I imagined it in my native County Antrim, and indeed some of the characters, like Shouting Sam, are drawn from the very colourful and loveable characters that were a feature of my childhood there.

Those were the days when packets of Woodbines could be bought for a few pence and many young people, not knowing the dangers of smoking, were inclined to have a 'pull' behind their parents' backs. Now, of course, things are different. We're all aware, as Cowlick points out, that smoking can be bad for our health. And so while Tapser is tempted to smoke not only cigarettes, but the pipe, young people of today will know better.

Likewise, they will be aware of the dangers involved in going on to a river or lake on such an unreliable means of transport as a makeshift raft, the craft which features in this original version. Just how foolhardy it is of Tapser and his friends to attempt such a voyage must be obvious.

The Devil's Cup, which they encounter in such a dramatic fashion, may be seen in a corner of the lake, or park dam as it's known locally, in the People's Park in Ballymena where my grandfather, Tom Smyth, was caretaker for many years, although the Cup is now railed over for safety and seems much smaller than it did when I was a boy.

As for the 'fairy fort' on Wariff Hill, that could be any one of several Norman forts, large earthen mounds that used to intrigue me as I stood on top of them and surveyed the countryside, as there was a common belief that from the top of one you could see the next and so on right across the North of Ireland.

As a boy I often attended the point-to-point races in the fields at Galgorm on the outskirts of Ballymena, and they were, as Tapser says, a powerful thing to watch.

At times, when writing, I may also have had in mind fleeting glimpses of Galgorm Castle. However, it's in Johnstown Castle in County Wexford that the unique features of the castle of the legend may be found, including the mysterious tower that stands in the woods a short distance away. Thanks to the hospitality of the staff of the Agricultural Institute which has been based there for many years, my family and I were able to visit Johnstown on a number of occasions, not only to research certain aspects of the story, but to enjoy the castle's beautiful surroundings, and it's there that the lakes, gardens and ornamental statues are also to be found.

Strange as it may seem for a story set in Northern Ireland, it was also from Wexford that I got the idea for the plot.

It all started with a report in one of our newspapers some

years ago, which stated that a valuable gold find, thought to have been buried for safety during the Rebellion of 1798, had been made in a County Wexford farm outhouse.

'The find,' it went on, 'of fifty-five gold coins (fifty-one guineas and four half-guineas) is being investigated by the National Museum. They were discovered by a farm worker while he was digging a cobblestone floor to lay a new one . . .'

The coins were the type known as George III spade guineas because of the spade-shaped shield on the back, and the report said that they dated from 1760 to 1798.

During subsequent research in the National Library in Dublin, I found that there had been a number of similar finds in Ireland down through the years.

Writing in the *British Numismatic Journal*, W. A. Seaby mentioned among other finds a tea-cup filled with French and Spanish gold coins, discovered in the thatch of an old house near Newtownards, County Down, in 1820, and coins to the value of thirty George III guineas at Castle Connel, County Limerick, in 1848.

More recently, he wrote, two gold hoards had been discovered in Northern Ireland. One was at Tullynewbane, Glenavy, County Antrim, in 1954, when a man carrying out reconstruction work on an old partly demolished cottage, found thirty-two gold coins on top of a cupboard; it was thought they might have fallen out of the thatch.

The coins — twenty-eight guineas and four half-guineas — were subsequently declared to be treasure trove, a payment was made to the finder, and the hoard placed on public exhibition at the Belfast Museum and Art Gallery.

The other find mentioned by Seaby was at Beechvale, Crumlin, County Antrim, in 1937. During digging operations on a farm eleven guineas were found, five dated between 1772 and 1781 and six of the spade type dated 1787 to 1791.

'The '98 Rebellion,' wrote Seaby, 'might appear to be

the most obvious cause for the non-recovery of the two Ulster hoards were it not that the breaks in the sequence of the coins are more consistent with the beginning of the French Revolutionary War in 1792, after which date thousands went into military or naval service, never to return to their homes.'

He then mentioned a most interesting romantic custom of those far-off days.

'It's worth noting,' he said, 'that three of the Tullynewbane coins were bent — one spade guinea of 1794 and two half-guineas of 1788 and 1789. These had almost certainly been used as love tokens, a practice much in vogue in the eighteenth century.'

And so the gold guinea became a very suitable symbol indeed for the story I had in mind, especially for the two tragic figures of '98, the young man and young woman my publisher, Rena Dardis, was to call the star-crossed lovers of the legend.

My intention in writing such stories for young people has been to give them books which they would not only enjoy, but from which they might learn a little. I've been heartened, therefore, to find that over the years *The Legend of the Golden Key* has formed the basis of numerous school projects and tours ... tours to museums to see their collections of gold guineas ... tours to Norman forts which are a common feature of the Irish countryside ... and tours to Newgrange in County Meath to see the great tumuli, the prehistoric burial mounds of our kings.

It's now my hope that new generations of young people will enjoy this full-length version of the story and visit those places too.

Tom McCaughren,
1988

1. THE SKIPPING SONG

It was a lovely summer's day, the sort of day you'd love
to have all the year round if you could. The swallows were
snatching flies from beneath the willow trees at the river's
edge, and Prince, my collie dog, was rooting for water-rats
down among the rushes.

It was quiet and peaceful, like it always is here in the
valley. The bombings and shootings we were hearing about
in other parts of Northern Ireland seemed as distant as the
call of the curlew.

Our big problem as we lazed up in the Willow Field
was what we were going to do for the rest of the holidays?

It was Cowlick who set us thinking about the legend.
The sound of the girls chanting their skipping song was
drifting up to us on the hot summer air from the roadway
near the houses.

'What are they singing?' asked Cowlick.

'Listen ...' I said, and when the girls started up their
skipping song again, I went over it too....

> *The man is dead*
>   *But life allows*
> *He'll run forever*
>   *Beneath the boughs*
> *And in his path*
>   *There lies the key*
> *To wealth, happiness*
>   *A bride-to-be . . .*

Cowlick looked puzzled. 'What is it?'

I shrugged. 'It's just one of the skipping songs here in the valley. Has been for generations, according to Old Daddy Armstrong. It's the legend — the Legend of the Golden Key.'

It's funny how you know something for years and never really think about it until someone else asks you. That's the way it was with the legend.

Cowlick hadn't heard about it before, even though he's my cousin, because he's from the glens. There had been two bombings in the glens, and he had been sent up to spend the summer holidays with us. His mother and father felt it would be safer. If they had known the trouble he was going to get into with us, they might have thought differently!

Cowlick ran his fingers through the cow's-lick curl that gives him his nickname and asked, 'What does the legend mean?'

'Something to do with the Kings,' Curly told him.

'The kings?'

I nodded. 'The Rochford-Kings, over at the castle. I heard Old Daddy Armstrong talking about it. I can't remember exactly, but it's some story that was handed down from one of their ancestors. It's supposed to be about a young girl who couldn't get married and a treasure that couldn't be found, and it's all tied up with some story about a ghost.'

'Treasure!' exclaimed Cowlick. 'Oh boy ... that's what I'd like to find ... buried treasure!'

'Wouldn't we all,' sighed Doubter. 'But don't forget, it's supposed to have happened ages and ages ago, if it ever happened at all.'

'Doubter's right,' I said. 'The Kings have even given up looking for it — or so they say.'

'Still,' said Cowlick. 'Buried treasure! It would be more fun looking for that than anything we've done so far — even if we didn't find it.'

The others nodded, and Curly added, 'It can't be much worse than what we've been doing. I mean, the summer's half over, and what have we done? Nothing!'

'Don't forget the gymkhana over at the castle,' I reminded them. 'That wasn't bad.'

'It wasn't great either,' Doubter remarked.

'It wasn't worth the money they were charging to get in,' said Totey.

I had to smile at the good of that. 'Go away, Totey!' I said. 'We didn't pay to get in, and you know it. Anyway, you're too small. They wouldn't have charged you even if you had gone in by the gate. And what about the yellow man? You all enjoyed it, didn't you?'

They couldn't argue with that. Yellow man is a home-made toffee we all love but usually the only time we get it is when we have a day out at the coast, or at the Lammas Fair in Ballycastle.

'And what about the ice-cream, and the lemonade?' I went on. 'And the jumping? That was good.'

'It wasn't as good as the point-to-point,' said Curly.

That was true, I had to admit. The point-to-point races that are held in this district every year are something special. Unlike the gymkhana there's always a long row of bookies giving odds on the horses and we love watching them with their hoarse cries, their arms waving and their big leather bags full of money. Then, when the races start, we're so close to the jumps the horses are almost sailing over our heads, there's mud flying everywhere, and everybody's shouting and waving and urging them on. That's a powerful thing to watch.

'Still,' I said, 'the jumping at the gymkhana was good too.'

'Did you see Simon Craig on that blood mare of his?' asked Doubter. 'Don't tell me you call that good jumping. I could do better myself.'

I said nothing, for I knew exactly what Doubter meant. Simon Craig hasn't a great way with horses. Indeed, I sometimes think when I see him on his blood mare that he needs riding-lessons more than we do.

'It's that horse,' said Curly. 'It's neither a carthorse nor a jumper, and he's always having trouble with it. I don't know why the Kings have him working around the place at all.'

'Felicity did well,' I said.

'Ah, and why wouldn't she?' said Doubter. 'Doesn't she run the riding-school over there. Sure she's out practising every day.'

'After that fall she took up in the plantation,' I said, 'I didn't think she would have been able to take part in the gymkhana at all.'

'That was a bad fall, wasn't it!' said Curly.

'What happened?' asked Cowlick.

'Mr. Rochford-King and Felicity were having a friendly race through the plantation,' I told him.

'... and she would have won too,' said Totey, 'if her horse hadn't thrown her.'

'They were jumping a fallen tree,' I explained. 'It didn't half give us a fright when we saw her go down like that. I think Mr. King got a bad fright too. But Felicity's a lot tougher than you would think, and she was back in the

saddle and away like the wind before anyone could help her.'

Just then we heard the clippity-clop of horses coming down the brae. I thought at first it was Gypsy Juno or some of his clan coming down from the Cottonbog Road, but then I saw it was Felicity.

'That's her now,' I told Cowlick. 'The others are pupils from her riding school.' As we watched them make their way down towards the houses, I explained, 'Felicity runs the riding-school to help Mr. Rochford-King and his mother pay for the upkeep of the castle, or so they say. Her father, Major Mortimer Boucher, is the Kings' estate manager.'

'Can anybody join the school?' asked Cowlick.

'Curly shrugged. 'It's not for the likes of us.'

Curly was right. We would have loved to be getting riding-lessons from Felicity, as we had all made up our minds a long time ago that when we grew up we were going to be knights, with swords and lances, and suits of shining armour, and fine prancing horses. But we weren't allowed into the estate, even to watch the others learning to ride.

'Why not?' asked Cowlick, when I told him.

'Poachers,' said Curly. 'They're afraid of poachers getting at their pheasants. Tapser will tell you about it. He's always mooching about in there with his father.'

'At least we eat what we catch,' I said. 'And anyway, my father says it's not poaching to take what's in the rivers and fields that God has made for everybody.'

'Ha! I dare you to tell that to Mr. Moxley, the new gamekeeper,' chortled Doubter.

'Or his big son Dan,' said Curly. 'I hear they're not too well disposed to visitors from the valley.'

Ignoring them, I watched Felicity and her pupils cross the stone bridge and ride on past the houses. Five or six of the girls who live round about had stopped their skipping and stepped into the side of the road until the horses went by. Then they started up their skipping song again . . .

> *The man is dead*
> *But life allows*
> *He'll run forever*
> *Beneath the boughs*
> *And in his path*
> *There lies the key*
> *To wealth, happiness*
> *A bride-to-be . . .*

2.   A TALE OF '98

With the legend still ringing in his ears, Cowlick was as excited as a hen on a hot griddle.

'That man you heard talking about it...' he said to me.

'Old Daddy Armstrong?'

'Do you think he'd tell us about it?'

'He might,' I told him. 'Then again, he might not.'

'If the berries on the bourtree were ripe it might be different,' said Doubter. 'We could bring him some to make wine. That always puts him in good humour. But all the bourtree is good for at the moment is making whistles, and they're no use to him.'

The others were watching me trying to smoke the pith of a withered branch of elderberry or, as we call it, bourtree. We had brought some back with us from the river where we had been looking for otters, but you just can't smoke the pith of bourtree. It's light and white and looks the same as cigarettes, but it's not.

'Tapser,' said Cowlick at last, 'you're the limit. I told

19

you, you can't smoke that stuff. Anyway, did nobody ever tell you smoking's bad for your health?'

I laughed and threw it away. 'I'll tell you what. We'll make whistles from the bark instead. From now on, every member of my gang has to have a bourtree whistle so that we can signal each other.'

They all agreed, and so we set about cutting and scooping.

Cowlick, I could see, was still thinking about the legend. 'Is there no other way we could get around Mr. Armstrong so that he would tell us about it?' he asked.

'We could ask him nicely, I suppose,' said Doubter, 'but if you lived around here you'd know you were only wasting your time.'

'Still,' persisted Cowlick, 'I'd love to hear the story. It's just like something you'd read in a book ... and after all, we don't have anything else to do. What about it?'

The others shrugged.

'All right,' I said, 'we'll ask him. But remember, he can be a bit odd. You wouldn't know what he'd say.'

'Seeing that Cowlick's a visitor, he might tell us about it,' said Curly, 'and we could take him up a nice trout, just to be on the safe side.'

It wasn't long before we had the whistles made. We gave them a toot or two to try them out. They worked great. Prince thought we were calling him and came racing up to us. Feeling highly pleased with ourselves, we crossed the road and went down the river towards the wooden bridge to catch some fish.

We walked along the edge of Mr. Stockman's cornfields, and selected a rocky pool not far from the bridge. While Doubter rolled up his trouser legs and hopped on to the nearest rock, I crossed the bridge to the Whin Hill side, rolled up my shirt sleeve another inch or two and hunkered down close to the bank. Doubter got down on his knees on the stone and poked his hand in around the side of it.

Then he craned his head up round and looked at me. I shook my head. Without a word he crossed to another rock and did the same. This time I nodded and crept along the bank a few feet. Doubter had just flushed a big brown trout from under the rock. It was my job to catch it.

I had seen it dart in below the bank on my side, and while I couldn't see it now, I knew exactly in my mind's eye just where it was. Slowly I slipped my arm in round the bank until I knew my hand was close to it. Then gently, very gently, I splashed the water against it with my fingers. All the time I kept going closer and closer, until in there in the darkness it couldn't tell the difference between my hand and the water. By this time it was lying straight across the palm of my hand. I couldn't see it, but I could tell. I moved up to its gills, and the next instant I whipped it out.

It's a nice trick that, when you get the hang of it, but it's not as easy as some people make out. Gypsy Juno showed us how to do it when we were only nippers and not allowed near the river at all. Of course, he's a pastmaster at it. He can lift a rabbit or a chicken just as handy. Any farmer in the valley will tell you that.

In next to no time we had two nice trout rolled up in big green dock leaves to keep them fresh.

'Well,' said Curly, 'if these don't make Old Daddy Armstrong tell us about the legend, nothing will.'

Next minute there was a shout from the top of the Whin Hill that nearly struck us dead with fright. Then we realised who it was. It was only Shouting Sam.

Sam's a bit odd — mad, some people say — and you would know him anywhere. He's long and thin, his trouser legs are tied with strips of sacking from the knees down, and he always carries a loud-speaker from an old gramophone together with an assortment of wires. That's how he gets his name, for he believes that when he throws the wires over a tree or bush, he can broadcast through the horn. Mind you, it's not everybody he'll broadcast to. He's a bit choosey that way. He never sends messages to anybody but Presidents, or Prime Ministers, or Kings and Queens.

'Hallo, hallo, hallo,' he bellowed through the horn. 'Calling Your Royal Highness the Queen of England. Calling your Royal Highness the Queen of England. Are you receiving me?'

Well, that's our Sam. That's the way he always starts, and thereafter, assuming apparently that he's being received loud and clear, it's his custom to launch into a discourse, as Mr. Stockman calls it, about letters and messages he thinks he has received from the Queen or whatever Head of State he's supposed to be talking to. It's always the same, and this time was no different from any other.

'But what on earth is he talking about?' asked Cowlick when we told him who the strange figure was.

'Your guess is as good as ours,' said Doubter. 'But I know one thing. We'll catch no more fish here after that racket.'

There was no doubt about that, so we gathered up our catch. By this time Sam had quite an audience, including my mother who was listening from the hen-pen gate, and Mr. Stockman who was working close by getting a field of corn ready for the combine harvester. Mr. Stockman has always been very good to people like Shouting Sam. He always feeds him when he's passing through and lets him use the Whin Hill for his broadcasts. Of course, some people say he's just as mad as Sam to be putting up with it, but we know Mr. Stockman; he's just over-kind.

Leaving Sam to his broadcasting, we headed down the river towards the fairy fort on Wariff Hill. We had another look at a clump of alder trees we were pretty sure were hiding otters, and from there we cut up over the fields to the plantation where Old Daddy Armstrong lives.

Shafts of sunlight flitted across our faces as we made our way through the trees towards the thatched cottage with its carefully-kept vegetable patch. We found the old man leaning over the green half-door, only one side of his braces up on his faded flannel vest, as usual, and smoking his stubby, silver-banded pipe.

When we emerged from the trees and skirted the vegetable patch, he gave us a wave with his pipe, and we knew he was in good form. He's a great man, and if you ever meet him you couldn't help but like him. He's got a beard the colour of his grey woollen waistcoat, and it nearly touches the point of his nose when he chews his tobacco, and he walks bent and uses a stick. Yet he's fairly active, considering he's nearly ninety if he's a day.

When he got too old to swing the blacksmith's hammer, Old Daddy Armstrong retired to his little white-washed cottage. However, he didn't take life much easier. He spends his days gardening and looking after his goats and hens, and, of course, making wine when the berries are on the bourtree. He sells a lot of the goats' milk and the wine to the Kings. Felicity calls for it every so often.

He was highly pleased with the trout, and invited us in.

Like all thatched cottages, Old Daddy Armstrong's is gloomy inside, but the glow of the peat fire, and the smell of a pot of potatoes he had just boiled to mash with meal for the hens, made it nice and homely. He eased himself into his creaking rocking-chair beside the big open fire-place, and asked Doubter, he being the tallest, to fill the kettle from the white enamel bucket on the table and hang it on the crook, while he relit his pipe.

When the kettle was on and his pipe was going and we were all seated around him on the stone floor, we got to talking.

'So you want to know about the Legend of the Golden

Key?' he asked. We nodded eagerly.

'You don't think it's an old wives' tale then — like some folks will have it?'

I gave Doubter a dig in the ribs with my elbow as I knew he was quite capable of saying he didn't believe a word of it and ruining the whole thing. He got my message and we all said no, we didn't think it was an old wives' tale.

Mr. Armstrong, who had been looking into the fire as if wondering whether he should confide in us or not, finally screwed up his face and said, 'Well, I'll tell you.' He thought for a minute. 'It goes back ... oh, nearly two hundred years.'

We whistled with surprise, hardly able to believe anything could go back that far.

'Indeed it does,' he went on. 'It goes back to the time of an ancestor of young Mr. Rochford-King, a man called Sir Timothy King. King's the family name of course. They're a very old family. They came here around the year 1600 as far as I can gather from Felicity. However, it was in later years that the legend was born. In fact, it was just before the 1798 Rebellion.

'Whether it was because times were so hard or not, I couldn't say, but Sir Timothy was a desperate miser and kept a tight fist on whatever gold he received for his services to the Crown. As fate would have it, he had a beautiful daughter, a lovely lass by all accounts — long silken hair, pretty as a picture. Things weren't too bad until the girl's mother died. When she was alive she saw to it that in spite of Sir Timothy's miserliness their daughter was kept in a manner befitting the lady she undoubtedly was. But when she died, things changed ...

'The story goes that Sir Timothy wouldn't allow his daughter to go anywhere or to entertain friends, and he was very stingy in the matter of clothes. He even paid off some of his servants and made her do the work. But she was beautiful, and she had a lover, a handsome young fellow with black hair, like Curly here. He was from somewhere nearby, but he had one big drawback — he wasn't one of the gentry. He had no money worth talking about, and money was the only thing that counted with Sir Timothy. He wanted his daughter to marry somebody with land and money — not that he ever gave her the chance.

'Well, to cut a long story short, he wouldn't hear tell of them getting married. Wouldn't hear tell of it at all! Then he had an idea. He was a great man for conundrums, or riddles. He was always making them up and offering people such and such if they could solve them. Of course, he always made the riddles so difficult it was almost impossble to solve them. It made him feel generous and smart at the same time.

'Anyway, he refused for a long time to give his daughter and this young fellow permission to marry. Then one day he sent for them. He told them he would give them permission to marry *and* provide his daughter with a dowry of half of all the golden guineas he owned *if* ... and it was a big if ...'

'If they could solve a riddle?' said Cowlick.

'Right — a riddle that contained three promises, one for each leaf of the shamrock, some people say. He told them that as a precaution against a possible attack by rebels, he had hidden half of his golden guineas outside the castle, but within the estate.'

'What are guineas?' asked Totey.

'Guineas were the most valuable coin they had in those days. They were made of solid gold and were worth one pound and one shilling, which was a lot then. Nowadays they would be worth a fortune. But as I was saying, Sir Timothy had hidden half of his golden guineas outside the castle, but within the estate, so that if there was a rebellion the rebels wouldn't find it. As a matter of fact, the Catholics and Presbyterians joined forces in the '98 Rebellion shortly afterwards and some of them were hanged when it was put down. They called themselves the United Irishmen.

'Anyway, he promised the young people his consent to marry, and the gold he had hidden, if the young man proved himself worthy by solving the riddle he had composed as the key to the hiding-place and thus to their marriage. You all know the words:

> *The man is dead*
> *But life allows*
> *He'll run forever*
> *Beneath the boughs*
> *And in his path*
> *There lies the key*
> *To wealth, happiness*
> *A bride-to-be . . .*

'The Legend of the Golden Key,' I said.

The old man nodded. 'The young fellow spent week after week, month after month, trying to solve the riddle. He searched every inch of the estate and every tree, including the trees over there in the family graveyard by the side of the castle, the animal graveyard at the back of it, and of course, the Gallows Tree. But no matter how much he searched, he couldn't solve the riddle of the running dead man that would lead him to the key.

'In the meantime, Sir Timothy, knowing fine well the lad wouldn't be able to solve the riddle, gave his daughter a present of a bracelet — a chain with a golden guinea attached — and told her when the right man came along he really would give her a handsome dowry of them. But those two young people were head over heels in love with each other.'

'Just like Mr. Rochford-King and Felicity,' I suggested.

The old man raised a bushy eyebrow and sort of looked

at me as if to say that wasn't any of my business, before
going on, 'As I was saying, they were very much in love
with one another, and the father's efforts to keep them apart
only brought them closer together.'

'Then why didn't they elope?' asked Curly.

'They could have tried, I suppose, but by all accounts
they didn't. You must remember that the people who owned
castles in those times also owned the best horses in the land
— they still do in many cases. They had to have the best
for themselves and their soldiers or they'd soon have been
defeated in battle. So what was the use in eloping? Sir
Timothy would have sent his best men after them on his
fastest horses and caught them, and, don't forget, they'd
have run a man through in those days for a lot less. Why
do you think that big tree at the back of the castle is called
the Gallows Tree? Many a poor soul was strung up there,
maybe for no more than stealing a sheep. So you can guess
what chance the young lad would have had if he was caught
stealing the lord's daughter!'

'What did they do then?' asked Cowlick.

'I suppose they decided they just couldn't live without
each other. Their favourite meeting-place was down by the
lake in the estate, and one night, hand-in-hand, they threw
themselves into the Devil's Cup. As you know, the water
flows into the Devil's Cup and disappears underground.
And the two of them were never seen again.'

'Then how did they know where they went?' asked
Doubter.

'Ah, they knew all right. You see, Sir Timothy had begun
to suspect that his daughter was having secret meetings with
this young man after he forbade them to see each other,
and as it so happened he checked her room that night and
found she was gone. He immediately ordered out his men
to look for them. All they found was the bracelet lying on
top of the wall above the Devil's Cup ... and they might

never have found that if they hadn't seen the golden guinea glittering in the light of a full moon.'

'What happened after that?' asked Totey.

'Well, the man must have been mad to treat his daughter the way he did in the first place, and after the young couple committed suicide, he went clean out of his head. Maybe it was only then he realised how much she meant to him. Maybe he really did have her best interests at heart when he told her he wanted her to marry well. Who knows? At any rate, it wasn't long before he was reduced to a raving lunatic. The remainder of his gold soon dwindled, and he died, to all intents and purposes penniless, having steadfastly refused to draw upon the gold he had hidden, let alone divulge its hiding-place to a single soul.

'Over the years,' added Old Daddy Armstrong, 'the castle has been renovated and parts of it rebuilt, but it has never given up the secret that Sir Timothy King took with him to the grave. Neither his brother, who inherited the castle, nor anyone since has been able to solve the legend. At some stage it was inscribed on Sir Timothy's tombstone over there in the family graveyard, and it can be seen there to this very day. It and the bracelet, which has been handed down from generation to generation, are the only known links with the hidden gold. Felicity wears the bracelet now as a present from Mr. Rochford-King to mark their engagement. So there you are. That's the story of the Legend of the Golden Key, as far as I know it.'

3. SEEING THINGS

We thanked Old Daddy Armstrong and left. Needless to say, we were no less thrilled with the story than Cowlick. At the same time it would have ended there had it not been for a chance remark Gypsy Juno made when we called up to see him on the Cottonbog Road a few days later.

We heard Juno yodelling long before we came to his camp. He's always yodelling and singing about horses and things, and my father says he must have seen too many singing cowboy pictures when he was small. Anyway, we found him busy skinning a rabbit he had strung up by the hind legs from a corner of the first caravan. It was a fine big rabbit with a broad back and we could see there'd be plenty of eating in it. As I said before, when it comes to catching a fish or snaring a rabbit, there's no one in the valley can match him, except maybe my father.

Prince bristled up to a yapping mongrel that had come out from under the caravan and Juno turned to greet us.

'Ha!' he smiled. 'If it's not my young buckos from below.'

'Hi Juno,' we replied and sidled up beside him.

A couple of tartan-shawled women were fixing a pot over an open wood fire and as we watched, Rosie, his mother, came down out of the second caravan.

'Have you not done that yet, Juno?' she shouted.

He gave us a wink and shouted back, 'A few minutes more, mother, just a few minutes more.'

'Saints preserve us,' she complained, 'we'll all die of the hunger this day if you don't get on with it.'

'Tapser, *alanna*,' he whispered, 'what can I do for you?'

Alanna is a word he always uses when he's talking to me or any of the boys. He told us once it's the Irish for darling and that they use it all the time when speaking to friends down in the South where he comes from.

'We want a badge for Cowlick,' I said, pointing to the ones that decorated the belt of his baggy blue trousers.

Juno makes these badges himself from scraps of copper he has left over after making little ornamental jugs and things for people's mantelpieces. The rest of us had already bought one each and we considered them good value for ten pence.

'Right,' he said, and wiping his hand on the side of his trousers he took down a tin box from just inside the doorway of the caravan. 'Take your pick, Cowlick. Usual price of course. Must live, you know.'

Cowlick picked through the badges until he found one in the shape of a horse's head that took his fancy.

'Now,' said Juno pocketing the 10p, 'what about your fortune? As a favour, I'll get mother to tell the fortune of all five of you for the price of one. How's that for a bargain?'

We shook our heads. We had no more money, and even if we had it wouldn't have made any difference, for there's something very peculiar about Rosie and that crystal ball of hers, and we didn't want anything to do with her.

Juno went on with his skinning. 'Ah, 'tis a great pity.' He turned to emphasise what he was going to say, with

his penknife. 'You know, there are fortune-tellers and fortune-tellers, but my mother, she's the best. There's not many have the power to penetrate the mysterious mists of time that veil the future. But she has, and no mistake.'

'I know, I know, Juno,' I said. 'It's not that we're doubting you. It's just, well ...'

'Okay, *alanna,* but you don't know what you're missing.'

We watched him working at the rabbit. After a few minutes he turned to us again and, pretending to be serious, said 'Tapser, you're sure you're not from a travelling family?'

I grinned and shook my head. Juno's always teasing me about that because of my red hair.

He smiled and said, 'Well, you've the hair of a travelling man and that's a fact.' Resuming the skinning, he asked, 'And what have you all been doing these past few days?'

'We heard the story of the legend,' Totey told him.

'From Mr. Armstrong,' explained Cowlick.

'Ha-ha, the Legend of the Golden Key.' Juno's a permanent fixture on the Cottonbog Road and very little goes on in the valley that he doesn't know about. He turned and we could see there was a twinkle in his eyes.

'You know,' he bent down and confided, 'I know the only man who has actually seen the running dead man — and lived to tell the tale!'

We laughed and asked him who?

'Shouting Sam!'

We shook our heads, and Doubter said, 'Sure you wouldn't want to be minding Sam. He's not half in it.'

'Maybe so,' said Juno. 'But he saw something over there in the estate not so long ago. Nothing will convince him he didn't.'

'You mean he thinks he saw a ghost?' I asked.

Juno shrugged to indicate our guess was as good as his.

'What did he say he saw?' asked Cowlick.

'You'll laugh ... but he says he saw a man rise up out

of one of the graves in the family cemetery and run off through the trees.'

We weren't quite sure whether to laugh or not. Then Cowlick asked, 'Did he say what the man was like?'

'Well, he did and he didn't. He said he was dressed sort of like himself, whatever he means by that.' Juno shook his head. 'I don't know. Maybe I should stop drinking with that man.'

'Ha! That'll be the day,' I laughed, knowing the wild drinking bouts the two always have every time Sam passes through the valley, and on that note we took our leave.

Cowlick could hardly contain his excitement, and was all for going over to the estate to investigate. Doubter, true to form, doubted if there was a word of truth in Juno's story and thought it would be a waste of time to bother.

To be truthful, I didn't know what to think, and neither did Totey or Curly. In the end Cowlick convinced us there was no harm in going to the estate and having a look, so off we went. We climbed up round the quarry dump and cut across Big Hughie McIlhagga's land, heading all the time for the belt of trees that runs around the back of it.

It was another warm day, and as we picked our way along the ditches a nice cool breeze blew in across the corn, waving it like a sea of green and gold.

'You might as well try and find a corncrake as find a grain of sense in any of Shouting Sam's stories,' Doubter remarked.

'True,' I said, knowing that corncrakes had disappeared from the valley since the farmers took to cutting the early meadow grass for silage. 'Still, I've been thinking about this story of the grave and one thing makes me wonder.'

'What's that?' asked Cowlick.

'Well, it's just that Sam can't have made any reference to it in his broadcasts or it would be all over the valley.'

'So what?' asked Curly.

'I don't know. Maybe he *did* see something and got such a fright he's scared to mention it.'

'And only told Juno about it when he was drunk,' suggested Cowlick.

'If he ever told him anything at all,' said Doubter. 'How do you know Juno's not just having us on? Sure *he* would tell a lie that would hang his own mother.'

There was no doubt about it. Juno did have the gift of the gab and it was hard to know when he was telling the truth and when he wasn't. Sometimes we wondered if he knew himself.

An urgent 'pink, pink' brought us to a sudden stop. We knew what it was, for we had often heard it before. It was a blackbird over in the belt of trees and it was madly alarmed about something. At the same time Prince gave a warning growl and I caught him and held him back. Thinking maybe the bird had been frightened by something down in the estate, we stole up behind the nearest hedge. When we got opposite to where it was 'pinking' away in the trees, I slipped my other hand over Prince's nose to keep him quiet.

The reason for the bird's alarm turned out to be a whitterick. My father always calls them whittericks, never stoats, and I must say I prefer it. Somehow whitterick seems a more fitting name for an animal that's so small and fast and deadly. This one had just killed a rabbit, and some of the boys were all for letting Prince go so that he could drive it off. Not me! I wasn't going to chance letting it get a grip on Prince's neck. I knew if it did it would never let him go until it killed him too.

Once I saw a whitterick jump on a long-legged heron over in the swamps at Wariff Hill. The heron screetched into flight and the whitterick hung on. Up and up they went, and big and all as the heron's wings were, they couldn't keep it in the air very long with that blood-thirsty little creature clinging to its neck like a leech. Finally — I remember it well — the big harmless bird fell lifeless to the ground.

Another thing too: I knew that if we took the rabbit the whitterick would follow us for miles, and I didn't want that. To tell the truth I was afraid of it. I've heard that whittericks sometimes hunt in packs, even call on each other for help and attack people. Whether that's true or not I don't know, but we decided to give this one a wide berth.

Once in the open field on the other side of the trees we felt a lot safer, and after some discussion we decided to go direct to the graveyard. From there we could cut across the estate to the river, and then double back home.

We climbed over a gap in the grey stone wall which runs around the estate and picked our way through a tangle of scrub ash and rhododendron bushes. Beyond that were tall oaks and beeches and we found it was nice and cool beneath them. It was quiet too. The only sounds were the cooing of wood pigeons and the cawing of crows high above us. There were few leaves on the ground and we were able to move along with hardly a rustle, which was just as well, seeing that my father and I hadn't tried out the new gamekeeper yet.

As we tip-toed up to the rusty iron gates of the graveyard, we fell quiet. Thin withered grass hung from its crumbling walls and long tangling briars grew all around the base of them. We knew one of the gates was stuck fast at the half-open position, and not knowing what to expect we went in.

At first glance the graveyard seemed deserted. Then to our surprise we saw a man digging at a grave in a corner beneath a clump of yew trees. From the description Old Daddy Armstrong gave us we guessed it was the grave of Sir Timothy King. But who was the man digging it up?

Almost before we realised what was happening, Prince bounded forward with a snarl and the man whirled to face him, the spade raised above his head ready to strike.

4. THE EMPTY TOWER

Well, there would have been skin and hair flying if I hadn't
given a shout in the nick of time. I rushed over and ordered
Prince to heel. Slowly the man lowered the spade. I could
see now he was stooped, and he had the sort of jaw that
made his stoop seem more pronounced. It stuck out as if
his top teeth went down behind his bottom teeth instead
of in front of them, if you know what I mean. But for
all that he was strongly built. The sleeves of his faded blue
shirt were rolled back to show powerful hairy forearms and
I remember noticing the large sweat marks around his
armpits as he lowered the spade.

'Gee, I'm sorry, mister,' I said, 'but you did take us a
bit by surprise.'

He dug the spade into the freshly turned soil, leaned an
elbow on the handle and regarded us.

I pointed to the grave, and as I did so I could see by
the legend on the headstone that it *was* Sir Timothy's. 'What
are you doing here anyway?' I ventured. 'Why are you

digging up Sir Timothy's grave?'

'Why shouldn't I be here?' he said sharply, his eyes switching from Prince to me and from me to the boys and back. 'I *am* a gardener here, or so they say.'

'Oh, that's right, you're ... Marcus, aren't you?' I had just remembered my father pointing him out to me once. He nodded.

'But why are you digging the grave?' asked Cowlick.

'For the same reason I've been digging all the other graves — to tidy them up.'

We followed the sweep of his hand and to our disappointment saw that all the other graves had indeed been dug over too.

'Now,' he went on, 'what, may I ask, are *you* doing here?'

'We were just ... a ...' We took a couple of embarrassed kicks at tufts of grass as we tried to think of excuses.

'All right, all right,' he said, 'but mind how you go. I don't want you trampling the flowers.'

'You mean you're not going to tell on us?' asked Curly.

'Now wouldn't you say I had more to do than be carrying tales — just so long as you don't tell anyone I said you could come in. Off with you now.'

Not quite knowing what to make of Marcus, we pretended to head for the boundary wall, doubled back and from a distance watched him through the graveyard gates. To our disappointment he continued to tidy up Sir Timothy's grave just as he claimed he had been doing when we had come upon him.

'What do you think?' I asked the boys.

'It's a bit of a coincidence that he was digging at just that grave,' said Cowlick.

'All the other graves were dug over too, just like he said,' observed Doubter.

'That could be just a cover-up,' I said.

'I know why he wouldn't tell on us,' said Totey. 'He's

a convict ... and convicts don't tell.'

'A convict?' repeated Cowlick incredulously, looking to me for an explanation.

I shrugged. 'Could be. They say the Kings do employ some ex-convicts, all right.'

'Goodness, what a set-up!' declared Cowlick.

'It was nice of him to say he wouldn't tell on us,' said Totey.

'That could be a cover-up, too,' I said. 'Look, if he has been doing something he shouldn't be doing, he might figure the best way to keep it quiet is to say he won't tell on us, so that we won't tell on him.'

'Exactly,' agreed Cowlick.

Just then we saw Marcus sink his spade into the soft earth and hurry away from the graveyard.

'Come on,' I whispered. 'Let's follow him.'

Crouching low, and taking cover every now and then behind trees and bushes, we kept Marcus in sight until he reached the avenue. When we got to it, however, he was nowhere to be seen. Totey seated himself on one of the large cannon-balls that line each side of the long winding avenue, and started poking at the sole of his Wellington boot.

'What's the matter, Totey?' I whispered.

'I think there's a thorn in my foot.'

'You choose a nice place to look for it,' said Doubter. 'Hurry, before someone comes.'

'Okay, I think I have it.'

'Listen,' said Curly, 'I think somebody *is* coming.'

He was right. We flung ourselves back in below a big rhododendron bush and I clamped a hand over Prince's nose. A few minutes later Mr. King and Felicity rode into sight.

Mr. King is more correctly known as Mr. Rochford-King, but we always refer to the family as the Kings because it's

handy and because it suits them, living in a castle and all. None of us had ever spoken to Mr. King, but we often saw him riding past our houses with the hounds. He sits the saddle well. He's thin and straight, sort of military-like. Indeed, I always got the impression that he was in the Army at one time or another, maybe as an officer. He has the sort of look on his face that tells you he'll stand for no nonsense.

As you can guess then, we were glad we hadn't burst out on to the avenue and frightened the horses. It would have been bad enough to have been caught trespassing, not to mention that. However, Mr. King and Felicity passed by, unaware that we were there.

We crossed the avenue and kept going until we reached the lake. There was still no sign of Marcus, so we concluded he must have gone up the avenue. We could hear the roar of the water spilling into the Devil's Cup, and as the water raging around the bottom of the giant stone bowl is a powerful thing to watch, we decided to have a look.

It always makes our hearts flutter when we lean over the wall between the iron spikes to gaze into the depths of the Devil's Cup, but this time was different somehow. This time as we watched the tons of foaming water swirling madly around the bottom before rushing underground, away forever from our sight, we couldn't help thinking about the pretty girl of the legend and her handsome curly-headed lover. In our mind's eye we could see them leaping hand-in-hand to their awful fate, and suddenly we felt quite dizzy and a little sick.

Turning away from the Devil's Cup, we cut back up through the estate, skirting the gardens and the farm buildings, and keeping a sharp look-out for anything strange. Over by the stables we saw Wilson Harper, the farm foreman, having a run-in with Simon Craig. Craig's blood mare was shying away from him as he jerked its halter and thrashed it with a sally rod, and we were delighted to see Harper grab the rod from him and give him a good talking-to. Craig, a big raw-boned fellow with deep-set eyes and long black hair sleeked back, glared at the foreman for a minute; but it takes a stout heart to stand up to Wilson Harper and Craig slunk away pulling the horse after him. It's nothing strange to see Craig ill-treating that horse of his. He lost his job with Big Hughie McIlhagga on the farm beyond for the very same thing. It's really more of racing blood than a farm horse. That's why it's so highly strung and called a blood mare.

We moved on, and then a short distance behind the castle we did come across something odd — something which on investigation we found to be odder still.

We were coming to an ancient stone tower that stands on its own among the trees, when, lo and behold, we saw the strangest figure walking up and down beneath the

Gallows Tree. He was a man of about sixty, with a drooping white moustache, and he was dressed in the most peculiar clothes. His hat was the sort Sherlock Holmes used to wear — a deerstalker I think they call it — and his trousers were those funny looking tweedy plus-fours that are tucked in below the knee. Yet it was the way he was acting that was really odd.

There he was, walking up and down, and one minute he was looking at the giant, ivy-covered trees, and the next he was looking at the ground. He had some sort of book in his hands, and now and then he would look at it and run a finger over some line he was reading. If it hadn't been for that outfit he was wearing, we might easily have taken him for one of those preachers we sometimes see on street corners up in Belfast or at the Lammas Fair; preachers who put the fear of God into us with sermons about hell-fire and damnation unless we repent. But if he was preaching he was completely unaware of his audience. Suddenly he whipped the book behind his back and, with a quick look around to see if anyone else was about, made a bee-line for the stone tower.

A minute or two later, a man wearing thigh-length waders and carrying a double-barrelled shot-gun appeared in the clearing. It was Mr. Moxley, the new gamekeeper. We held our breath — and Prince. Luckily he didn't spot us, and when he had gone we settled down to wait for the strange figure to reappear from the tower.

Half an hour passed and still there was no sign of him. Finally, we elected Cowlick to steal up and have a quick look through one of the window slits to see what he was doing, for we were sure he was up to something. I'd have gone too, but my red hair is easily seen, and anyway I had to hold Prince.

Off went Cowlick, using the trees for cover, until he was at one of the window slits. He peeped in and then he did

a most surprising thing. He went round to the doorway, took a quick look inside and waved to us to join him. Thinking something was wrong, we ran over to him and looked inside. The tower was empty!

We were baffled. The strange figure had gone into the tower. We saw him enter, and we didn't see him leave. Yet we could see for ourselves there was nothing in it now, apart from an assortment of gardening tools. There was no doubt about it, there was something very odd here. We all agreed on that as we headed for the boundary wall. That was when we walked straight into the gamekeeper's son, Dan. We were so busy talking about what had happened that we didn't see him until we nearly bumped into him. He's a big fat fellow with a surly scowl on his podgy cheeks, and he held a half-eaten apple in one of his hands.

'Well, well,' he sneered, 'what have we here — one, two, three, four, *five* trespassers, and a dog. Poaching!'

'Who says we're poaching?' demanded Cowlick.

'So you're the ringleader...'

'I'm the leader,' said I, stepping forward, 'and don't you forget it.' You have to talk tough like that when you're the leader. I was shaking in my boots, for he's a huge fellow, but naturally I couldn't show it.

Dan Moxley wasn't unduly impressed. He took a big loud bite of the apple, and with his mouth half-full, said, 'Don't worry, I won't forget it. I know who you are. My father's the new gamekeeper here and I'm going to tell him. Now we know who overturned the headstones in the graveyard.'

I looked at the boys, and they looked at me. Fortunately they kept their thoughts to themselves. I turned to Moxley. 'I don't know what you're talking about. Anyway, your father can't do a thing unless he catches us.'

'Well, I've caught you,' he said, and stepped forward to take hold of me.

It's funny how some people take a dog for granted. It's

a big mistake too, as Dan Moxley found out the minute he reached for me. Prince didn't move. He didn't even open his mouth. The hair went up on the back of his neck, and his top lip curled to show his teeth, and he gave a snarl that made Moxley snatch back his hand in double-quick time.

'Keep that brute under control,' he warned, but he should have known better than to point at Prince at a time like that. The collie took one step forward and those gleaming white fangs gave one snap. Moxley immediately pulled back his hand, dropping the apple as he did so, and backed up against a tree. 'Call that brute off,' he cried, 'or it'll be the worse for you.'

'Not on your life,' I said. 'He's staying right where he is — to make sure you do the same.' I could see big smiles breaking out over the faces of the others. 'Stay, Prince, stay, boy,' I ordered, and Prince, still bristling and snarling, sat back on his hind legs just in front of him.

'Happy dreams, Dan,' chaffed Curly as we left.

'Yes, we'll be seeing you,' I laughed.

'Maybe sooner than you think,' he retorted, 'and maybe you won't have your dog to help you.'

We laughed and went on towards the bridge on the boundary of the estate where we knew there was a stile. Leaving the river, we began climbing back up towards the trees at the back of Big Hughie McIlhagga's place. When we had put a good field's length between us and the estate, I took out my bourtree whistle and called Prince. Away down in the estate we heard an answering bark, and then he streaked up towards. us. As we patted him for his good work, Dan Moxley's parting words ran through my mind.

How true they turned out to be!

5. THE MISSING CHARM

Convinced now that there was something peculiar going on at the castle, we kept a close watch on it for the rest of the week. However, we saw nothing else that struck us as being unusual. Marcus finished tidying up the family graveyard. We also saw him go into the stone tower a number of times, but unlike the strange figure in tweeds he always came out again with tools and went about his gardening, so we didn't know quite what to make of him.

Each time as we lay in hiding among the rhododendron bushes not far from the tower, we discussed the man in tweeds at length. Who could he be? we wondered. Finally, Totey voiced the thought that had crossed our minds more than once when he piped up to say he thought the strange figure was the ghost of the dead man of the legend. For once I agreed with Doubter. Maybe the man *did* disappear, but we just didn't believe he was a ghost. After all, we had seen him in broad daylight. Cowlick and Curly, on the other hand, weren't prepared to discount any possibility.

As a result we decided to give Old Daddy Armstrong another call and ask him to tell us about the ghosts of the castle, especially the running dead man.

As it happened, we got word that very night that the old man wanted to see us. Mr. Stockman had seen him up at the plantation during the day and gave Cowlick and me the message when he came over to see my father in the evening. What Mr. Armstrong wanted to see us about, we couldn't imagine. We could hardly wait to find out, so early next morning, after grabbing a bit of breakfast, we collected the boys and hurried up Mr. Stockman's back lane.

It had been raining during the night and the grass and the leaves were hanging with rain as we made our way through the plantation. The old man was leaning on the half-door, waiting, and we wondered why he was so anxious to see us.

In fact, it was none of the things we thought it might be, but something much more exciting. Apparently Mr. King and Felicity had dropped by the cottage the previous day. They told him that during the gallop through the plantation before the gymkhana, when Felicity had taken the fall, she had lost the bracelet of the Legend of the Golden Key. They had been over the ground a number of times themselves, and had failed to find it. It was terribly important that they should get it back, and as a last resort they had called in the hope that he might have found it.

The old man, of course, hadn't seen it either, but being so fond of Felicity he wondered if we might do him the favour of having a look for it.

Needless to say, it was no favour as far as we were concerned. We were delighted. He reminded us what the bracelet looked like — a gold coin on a gold chain — and off we went. We fine-combed the spot where Felicity had been thrown from her horse. Then we searched a good stretch of the plantation, and indeed a fair bit more besides. Back and forth we went, the five of us all spread out so that we wouldn't miss it. All morning we looked, and after we had our lunch we took up the search again, but there was no sign of the bracelet. Finally, that afternoon, we reported our failure to Old Daddy Armstrong.

He was working in his vegetable patch when we arrived, and when we told him we hadn't found the bracelet, he pushed himself up with his stick and invited us into the cottage. He said he was meaning to go in and make himself a cup of tea anyway, and that by the looks of us we could do with a cup too. How right he was. By this time we were tired and wet and very disappointed that we hadn't been able to rescue Felicity from her difficulty or make any headway in the mystery of the Legend of the Golden Key.

Seated in our favourite positions around the open fire, we told Mr. Armstrong about our search, what ground we had covered and how thoroughly we had done it. As we talked, he sat there listening, puffing his pipe and looking through lungfuls of blue pipe smoke at the glowing peat fire. When we had finished, he leaned forward, knocked his pipe against the hob, blew through it and put it back in his pocket.

'Well boys, you couldn't have done much more than that,' he wheezed. 'But Felicity and his lordship will be powerful disappointed.'

'What sort of coin exactly did you say was on the bracelet?' Cowlick asked him.

'It's what was known in those days as a spade guinea.' The old man rummaged around in his coat pocket until he found a piece of paper. 'They wrote down the description for me here. Listen carefully now so you'll not mistake it if you do happen to come across it.'

'On one side it has the words *Georgivs III* and *Dei Gratia* written around the head of King George.' He showed us these words as he couldn't pronounce them very well and I didn't blame him. 'On the other side is a spade-shaped shield with a crown on top of it. The shield is divided into four parts, with a different emblem in each, including the English lions and the Irish harp, and just below it is the date — 1793.'

He thought for a moment, then added, 'It's a funny thing about the bracelet, but they say it has brought a certain amount of good luck to all who have worn it down through the years. I suppose each generation, having failed to solve the legend, has hung on to it in the hope that through it they might some day find the treasure. So you see how important it is that they should find it?'

'If it's so important, why did the Kings let it go out of the family in the first place?' asked Doubter. 'I mean, why did they give it to Felicity?'

'Sure it's not going out of the family. Young Mr. Rochford-King and Felicity are in love with each other, just as much as the young couple I was telling you about in the legend, and some day they'll get married. In the meantime they thought that if she was to wear the bracelet it might bring them luck.'

'Why don't they get married now?' asked Totey.

'Ah, that's a good question, Totey m'boy,' the old man went on. 'It's not that they don't want to get married now. They do, but it's not as simple as that.'

He thought for a moment as if wondering how he would explain it, and continued, 'You see, it takes an awful lot of money to run a castle nowadays. It's not like the past when noblemen got gifts of castles for favours rendered to the Crown and lived off the fat of the land. Nowadays they have to pay rates and taxes like everybody else, and a castle costs a fortune to keep up. Not only that, but I hear they had to pay an awful lot of death duties when the father died. Young Mr. Rochford-King and his mother are being put to the pin of their collar to make ends meet, and he doesn't think Felicity and himself should get married until he can give her the sort of life he'd like to give her.'

'What is he going to do?' asked Cowlick.

'He's been trying a lot of things to add to the income they get from the farm. The riding-school Felicity runs for him is one of them. Then there are the gymkhanas. But it hasn't been enough. I saw in the local paper that he's thinking of throwing the castle open to the public now. He'd charge so much a head for letting people look at his collection of armour and swords and paintings and all that sort of stuff. Mind you, it's a big step throwing your home open to the public like that, and I hear the mother's not very fond of the idea. But it's either that or sell some of their paintings, which are family heirlooms and worth a good bit I'd say.'

'What else did the paper say?' I asked.

'Nothing much. But there was a nice picture of the pair of them ...' He twisted around and rummaged behind the cushion of his chair. 'Ah, here it is. Man, they're a good-looking young couple.' He passed the paper down to us and we looked at it and nodded. Then something struck me.

'Wait a minute!' I exclaimed. 'When was that photograph taken?'

Mr. Armstrong scratched his head and thought for a moment. 'Let me see now. I think Felicity said it was taken the night of the gymkhana — why?'

'Because in the photograph she's wearing the bracelet — look!'

'Be the hokey, you're right, Tapser,' he wheezed. 'Now why didn't I see that?'

'But what does that mean?' asked Cowlick.

'It means,' I said, 'she couldn't have lost it when she fell off her horse in the plantation, as she told Daddy

Armstrong, because the gymkhana was held *after* that, and the picture shows she still had it the night of the gymkhana.'

'Maybe she didn't lose it at all,' suggested Doubter.

'Now hold on there, young fellow,' said the old man. 'That's not fair to Felicity. If she says she lost it, she lost it. Maybe that fall she took up here was the only time she could think of when she might have lost it. Then again, maybe she just thinks she has lost it, while in fact she may only have mislaid it.'

I could see Old Daddy Armstrong had complete faith in Felicity. To be honest, I didn't know what to think. In spite of my great affection for her, I couldn't help wondering if, for some reason, she just wanted to make it look as if she had lost the bracelet in that fall. I know it wasn't very loyal of me, but I couldn't help it. I could see the boys didn't know what to make of it either.

Knowing what was going through our minds, the old man closed the subject by directing us to take down the kettle which was plouting on the crook, and make the tea. By this time our wet socks were steaming and our faces were flushed from the heat, so we were ready to push back from the fire anyway.

Curly unhooked the kettle, while Doubter and Cowlick took down half a dozen big blue-and-white striped mugs from the row of hooks on the dresser. It was difficult to judge the amount of tea that was needed for so many of us, and it surprised nobody when it turned out to be so strong you could have stood on it. Even so, it didn't seem half strong enough for Old Daddy Armstrong. We were quick to see him pour something into his mug from a silver hip-flask. He said it was his medicine, but we knew better. It was whiskey; we could smell it. He has a great appetite for a man of his age. Indeed he's always saying he could eat a dog if he could get his fork into it! At the same time we guessed maybe the whiskey was something he forgot

to tell us about when he said potatoes and eggs were the
secret of his long life.

When he had drained his mug, we watched him take a
plug of Mick McQuaid tobacco from his waistcoat pocket.
He cut several slivers into his grubby palm, and rubbed
them with his thumb. Then, using his forefinger, he
funnelled the tobacco into his pipe from his cupped hand.
It always fascinated me the way he did that, and I was
just thinking I might try the pipe myself some day when
Cowlick said, 'But you didn't tell us about the ghost. There
is a ghost connected with the legend, isn't there, Mr.
Armstrong?'

The old man was lighting his pipe now, and he sucked
and puffed until a long yellow flame was leaping from the

bowl. Then he pressed the wriggling tobacco with his finger and leaned back. 'Aye, there is a story about a ghost all right.'

'The ghost of the running dead man?' suggested Cowlick.

He shook his head. 'Nobody could ever figure out who or what the running dead man was. Of course there's some who say it's the ghost of Sir Timothy and that his footsteps can be heard in the castle in the dead of night. Whether that's so, or if he *is* a ghost, nobody knows for sure, for nobody's ever seen him that I heard tell of. No, the ghost story arose from the drowning I was telling you about. They say that every time there's a full moon you can see the ghost of the girl rising like a soft light from the spray of the Devil's Cup, her long white dress billowing behind her, her silken hair blowing in the breeze, and her pale face mirrored in the rushing water of the lake.

'They say, too,' he added, 'that it has been seen to float across the Cottonbog, aye, as far as the fairy fort on Wariff Hill where, tradition has it, the young lovers first met.'

'Do you believe it?' asked Doubter.

'Well, I'm not saying I do, and I'm not saying I don't. But there's some of the castle staff who swear they've seen it. The Phantom of the Lake they call it.'

I could just imagine it. Mind you, I don't usually put much stock in ghosts or phantoms or things like that, but sitting there in Old Daddy Armstrong's gloomy cottage gazing into the glowing peat fire, I could just imagine the phantom, a sorrowful, eerie figure floating up among the trees of the estate. I don't mind telling you, it sent a shiver right down my back. I suppose most of us were imagining the same, when Cowlick suddenly said, 'Was Marcus ever in jail?'

Old Daddy Armstrong closed one eye, screwed up his face at Cowlick and regarded him for a minute before saying, 'Now I don't know what you're up to, young fellow-me-lad, but if you're thinking that being in jail makes Marcus any worse than any of the other workers in the estate, you've another think coming.'

'Does that mean Marcus *was* in jail?' asked Cowlick.

'As it so happens he was — a long while back. Then, so was the farm foreman, Wilson Harper, and maybe half a dozen others I could mention, if I had a mind to, which I haven't.'

Cowlick was puzzled. 'How come?'

'It's very simple,' the old man told him. 'When people are released from jail they can find it very difficult to get a job. So Mr. Rochford-King gets an allowance from the authorities for taking some of them on. It all helps to pay for the castle. But don't get the idea they're surrounded by criminals over there. They only take on men they're satisfied want to make a fresh start and none of them have ever let the family down, at least not that I've ever heard of. I thought, Tapser, you'd have told him all about that.'

I scratched my head. 'I knew there was something like that going on. I wasn't sure.'

'Was Simon Craig ever in jail?' asked Totey.

'No, not as far as I know. Why?'

'I think anyone who's as bad to a horse as he is should be in jail.'

The old man smiled. 'As a person who has spent his life around horses, Totey, I'll agree with you there.'

'Just one more thing, Mr. Armstrong,' said Cowlick. 'If I was to tell you we saw a man wearing a deerstalker hat and plus-fours, what would you say?'

'Did he have a white walrus moustache by any chance?'

We nodded, and he told us, 'I thought as much! I'd say you've been trespassing in the estate ... that's Major Mortimer Boucher, Felicity's father.'

6. FAIRY GOLD

Old Daddy Armstrong had no idea of the surprise he gave us when he told us who the strange figure in tweeds was, and while it cleared up one point for us it only added to our puzzlement.

From the way Major Boucher had been acting beneath the Gallows Tree, we concluded that he was either mad or up to something. Being estate manager, he could hardly be mad. What then was he up to? Had it anything to do with the strange happenings in the family graveyard, or with the mystery of the missing bracelet? Moreover, what did all or any of these occurrences have to do with the Legend of the Golden Key?

Maybe, we thought, it was our imagination, but we felt they had a direct bearing on the legend. Doubter, to give him his due, was convinced of it too. So we continued our vigil in the grounds of the castle.

To our great disappointment, our vigil was once more in vain. We saw nothing else worth talking about, and I'm afraid it wasn't long before our enthusiasm began to flag. Soon we drifted back into our old ways. The adventure we had hoped for was over, it seemed, before it began.

As my father often says, things aren't always what they seem, and it was certainly true in this case. Unknown to us, the scene of the mystery of the Legend of the Golden Key was about to change, and we were to be drawn into it again in a most unexpected fashion.

We continued to keep a look-out for otters on the river, and sure enough, we finally spotted their tell-tale droppings around the alder trees. At that spot the water swirls around the rocks in a deep pool, and we knew it was an ideal place for otters. We also knew we wouldn't see them in the daytime, so we arranged to meet at the stone bridge after dark.

Having made our excuses, we all slipped out at the appointed time. For a moment Cowlick and I paused in the darkness to debate whether or not to bring Prince, but in the end decided against it in case he might scare the otters away.

The night couldn't have been better. There was a full moon and it lit up the river just nicely. Excited at the prospect of seeing the otters, we slipped down through the hedge at the side of the bridge and made our way cautiously along the river.

It's odd how everything looks different at night, even when there's a full moon. The Whin Hill, familiar to us during the day, was now a strange dark blob sticking up into the night sky. So was Wariff Hill up ahead, but that's always a scarey sort of place, even in the day-time. The bank of the river didn't seem the same either. We thought we knew every bump and hollow of it, but we took a good few empty steps, and some wet ones in the marshy ground beside the cornfields.

When we reached the area of the alders, we crawled quietly through the clumps of scrub and rushes until we were peering over into the pool. Trying to breathe so nothing would hear us, we settled down to wait. Everything was quiet, save for the water swirling around the rocks, and what seemed to us the uncommonly loud beating of our hearts. The moon was still clear of cloud and casting soft light on the water.

Suddenly we heard a plop nearby, but nothing came of it. Probably a water-rat slipping off somewhere, we thought. A few minutes later we were startled by a rustle in the undergrowth behind us, but it didn't come to anything either.

We began to get restless. Doubter whispered that we were wasting our time. I shushed him and told him to have patience. We fixed our eyes on the water again, and that was when we saw them. First one streak in the pool, then another. We nudged each other and held our breath. Two or three dark shapes ran up the flat rocks on the far side. Faster than our eyes could follow, they were in the water again, swimming round and round the pool, turning over and under like playful seals. Probably a bitch otter and two young, we thought.

We didn't get the chance to have a better look at them. Almost before we knew it, they were gone. At the same time we became aware of something we hadn't noticed before, something which nearly struck us dead with fright. There, gliding around the fairy fort on Wariff Hill, was a ghostly white light. Too terrified to speak, we could only watch. Then the thing seemed to move slowly down the hill towards us.

Well, we had heard too much from Old Daddy Armstrong not to know what it was.

'The phantom!' I choked, finding my voice at last.

That was all that was said. With one accord we turned and fled. I don't know how we did it, but we covered the ground back to the road a lot quicker than we ever did in daylight. Expecting the phantom to be on us with every step and stumble we took, we shoved each other up through the hedge and didn't stop until we were in our beds with the blinds down and the lights on.

Things like that always seem different in the clear light of day. When we met next morning we all felt a bit foolish and a lot braver. We chided each other about who had run the fastest, and laughed at each other to try and make it appear we hadn't been as scared as we really were. Before long we were assuring each other that there weren't any such things as phantoms or ghosts, and that if we went up to Wariff Hill now, in the daylight, we'd probably find a simple explanation for the whole thing.

Half believing that, we set off for Wariff Hill immediately after lunch, taking good care this time to bring Prince.

Wariff Hill is a strange place at the best of times. It's covered with wild rambling nut-trees and surrounded by swamps, except for one high field that juts out like a giant finger towards the castle. You can't approach it by that field, as more often than not Big Hughie's bull is grazing there, so you have to go through the swamps to get to it. Sometimes, without warning, a heavy mist comes down on the swamps in a most ghostly fashion and curls around the hill like a giant smoke ring. The shrubbery, clinging to the slopes as if cloaking it in some strange secret, adds to the eerie atmosphere of the place. The only bare patch is the fort on top, for all the world like the home of the fairies, guarded by a tangled mass of tripping briars and branches and sagging swamps ready to swallow anyone foolish enough to be deceived by their rich coat of dark green grass.

Wariff Hill is the haunt of owls, badgers, foxes and goodness knows what. Yet it's as quiet as a tomb. It's an uneasy quiet, and you can never help feeling that it's just temporary, and that it will only last until unseen eyes see you depart. Maybe then you'll understand why we seldom, if ever, venture there, even for hazel-nuts, and why now,

in spite of our brave talk, we kept close together as we headed for it.

Soon the cultivated fields were behind us, and we were going down a stony slope to a meadow containing two old dams that had been used for steeping flax in the days when farmers in the valley grew flax for the linen mills. To the left of the meadow, on a rise, we could see the crumbling outline of what was once a farmstead, and beyond it — Wariff Hill.

A rusty iron gate lay tilted at the entrance to the lane, which was now a tunnel of overgrown hedges. We climbed over it and without a word wended our way through the nettles and other weeds. It was gloomy in there. Nothing moved except the tiny midges that flitted about our heads, irritating our ears and faces. If there were birds in the trees they were keeping quiet, and the leaves were too thick to see them. We half expected to hear a flock of wood pigeons flapping out of the ash-trees or see a blackbird go screeching down along the hedge, but everything was quiet.

The farmyard was the most overgrown place we had ever seen. What had once been hedges were now huge masses of sprawling bushes and trees. Nettles as big as ourselves grew in great clumps everywhere, and the smell of their stinging leaves was all through the air. The roofs of most of the buildings had fallen in, and where bits of rotten thatch still clung to the crumbling stone walls, more nettles stretched high.

We couldn't but wonder who had once lived and worked there, and why they had left. For my part, I could imagine an elderly woman with grey hair tied back in a bun, sitting at a turf fire in the dark kitchen, and in the yard an aged farmer with a drooping grey moustache, working at something he had lost interest in many years before. How, I wondered, had the farm come to be empty? After all, the couple must have had some family. Then I looked on past the house towards Wariff Hill. Somehow the hill, the swamps and the ruins seemed to be part of the same silent desolation.

There was a strange, frightening atmosphere about the place, an eerie feeling we couldn't fathom. Perhaps it was the unnatural silence, a deathly silence, and yet a silence which seemed to be alive with the spirit of the past. It was almost as if, somehow, the people who in times gone by had lived and died there, were forever watching over this long forsaken place. We stared around us for a moment, then hurried on.

The yard opened on to a meadow covered with white, sweet-scented clover. At the end of the meadow we could see Big Hughie's bull in the one field that runs up to the hill. There was no access to the hill that way, so we entered the soft, evil-smelling swamps. Knowing that one wrong step could mean disaster, we had to be extra careful and light-footed. Even so, we hadn't gone very far when Totey stepped in up to one of his knees. However, he was lucky. He didn't even lose his shoe.

We were making good progress when a harsh scream somewhere up ahead brought us to a sudden halt. We couldn't have been more surprised if the swamps had opened up and swallowed us. Back we stepped, trampling on each other as we did so. Cowering down, we peered through the reeds and long grass. We could see nothing. We were trembling with fright, but we had to move as the swamp water was beginning to creep up around our feet. Then we saw it. It was only an owl! We laughed, and as the bird flapped its big brown wings and glided out of sight, we pushed on and crossed into the firm, whin-covered ground at the foot of the hill.

We rested for a moment on the fringe before starting the climb, to give Totey a chance to wring out his wet sock and clean his shoe. Doubter reached up, seized a branch and plucked a handful of hazel-nuts to test them. They were still milk-white and tasteless. We moved on.

The hill is so completely covered with nut-trees that it's almost dark in the maze of twisting avenues beneath. Wild rose and honeysuckle entwine themselves through many of the trees, weaving them tight. You would think a place like that, quiet and dark, would be a perfect sanctuary for birds, but there wasn't a movement or a sound, except for the occasional crack of a twig or the swish of a branch as we made our way deeper into the hill.

Suddenly a ghostly sound froze us in our tracks once more. We listened. There it was again. The others were beginning to back down the path, and I knew they would break into a run at any moment.

'For goodness sake,' I whispered, 'it's only a fox.'

With the thought of the phantom fresh in our minds we were on edge. Luckily I remembered I had heard the noise once before when I was out hunting with my father. It was only the hiccup of a vixen calling her cubs to safety.

Prince knew what it was too, and it was all I could do to keep him from going after them. Normally I would have let him go, but I wanted him with us up at the fort, just in case.

Soon we emerged into the daylight of the open space at the top and cautiously scanned the fort. There was nothing unusual, as far as we could see. Plucking up courage, we picked our way through the bracken and the briars until we had made our way right around it. There was still no sign of anything out of the ordinary, so we climbed to the top. Shading our eyes from the sun, we viewed the countryside. We could see for miles around — the valley stretching away into a haze of blue, and the castle rather closer than we had imagined.

'What were forts used for in olden days anyway?' asked Curly, not expecting an answer from anyone in particular.

'Castles,' said Cowlick.

'Castles?' I said. 'Sure they're only big mounds of earth.'

Cowlick nodded. 'That's all they are now, but I read a book about them once. According to it, the Normans made them hundreds of years ago and built wooden castles or forts around the top of them. Of course that part of them has all gone now, but the mounds are still called forts.'

There was silence as we pictured Normans with swords and shields defending their forts against waves of Irish warriors.

Doubter brought us back to earth when he shrugged and said, 'I don't understand it.'

'Understand what?' I asked him.

'The phantom. I mean, there's nothing to show that anybody or anything has ever been up here.'

He was wrong. At that precise moment, whatever look I gave, I spotted something glittering in the sunlight in a web of withered ferns at the foot of the mound.

'Look!' I cried. 'Over there!'

Quickly we slithered down to investigate.

'What is it?' asked Totey as I reached into the ferns.

'Some sort of coin,' I said. 'It's partly wrapped in paper.'

I spread the paper out in the palm of my hand to reveal a glittering golden spade guinea.

'It's from Felicity's bracelet,' gasped Curly.

I shook my head. 'It's the same all right, but it can't be. There's no hole in it for the chain.'

'Then it's . . .' Doubter stopped. 'But it can't be!'

'It is,' I said. 'It's part of the lost treasure. It has to be.'

'What does it say on the paper?' asked Cowlick.

I slipped it from under the coin and read out the words that were scribbled on it . . .

> *The man is dead*
> *But life allows*
> *He'll run forever*
> *Beneath the boughs*
> *And in his path*
> *There lies the key*
> *To wealth, happiness,*
> *A bride-to-be . . .*

As I finished reading it, the others whispered with one voice, 'The Legend of the Golden Key!'

I nodded. All of a sudden Wariff Hill had become even quieter than before.

7.   THE STRANGEST THING

When we got home, and I must confess we didn't dally
after picking up the coin, we decided it was time we sat
down and had another good talk about things.

'One thing for sure,' I said to the boys, 'there's something
very peculiar going on.'

They nodded.

'Do you think that guinea is really from the treasure?'
asked Cowlick.

'I don't know where else it could have come from,' I
said. 'It's the exact same as the one on the bracelet. Then
again, if somebody has found the treasure why should they
take one guinea, wrap it in the legend, and leave it up at
the fairy fort?'

'Maybe,' said Totey, 'the phantom left it there — as a
sort of token.'

Not wanting even to admit to ourselves that such a thing
was possible, we ignored him.

'I tell you what,' suggested Cowlick. 'Let's recap, the

way the detectives do on the telly, and see if we can make any sense of it.'

'Right,' I said. 'Now where will we start?'

'With the legend,' replied Curly. 'Where else?'

'Okay,' I said, '... the legend. Nobody's ever been able to solve the riddle of it, and so over the years nobody's been able to find the treasure. We know from Old Daddy Armstrong that Mr. King and Felicity want to get married, but that he's nearly broke and they'd give anything to find the treasure. So he makes her a present of the only known link with it, apart from the legend — the bracelet. Now, the bracelet has always been a lucky charm for all the women who wore it, and the Kings hoped that by being worn again it would bring them luck in their search for the lost treasure. But they've had no luck. The bracelet has disappeared in circumstances which make us wonder whether it has been lost or deliberately mislaid.'

'Maybe,' said Curly, 'Felicity has really mislaid it, but is scared to tell Mr. King — in case he'd think she's very careless and maybe even break off their engagement.'

'And maybe her father was looking for it the day we saw him acting funny in the estate,' said Totey.

'More likely he was looking for the treasure!' said Cowlick.

'But why should he be so secretive about it?' argued Doubter. 'After all, he *is* the manager of the estate, and can do what he likes. I see no reason in the world why he should go around dodging people as if he was a trespasser.'

'Well, I see no reason why he should go around dressed like Sherlock Holmes,' I said, 'but he does.'

'And the way he disappeared,' said Totey.

Curly nodded. 'I wonder how he got out of the tower without us seeing him?'

I shook my head.

'Do you think he might be afraid of some of the ex-convicts going after the treasure too?' asked Cowlick.

'If they're not already after it,' I said. 'You saw Marcus yourself at Sir Timothy's grave.'

'What do you think Shouting Sam saw at the grave?' asked Totey.

'More to the point,' I said, 'what did *we* see gliding around the fairy fort?' I weighed the guinea in my hand. 'And how did this spade guinea come to be there?'

'You know,' said Curly, 'it's a funny thing, that . . .'

'What is?' I asked him.

'The way we found it. I mean, according to Old Daddy Armstrong the guinea on the bracelet was found when Sir Timothy's men saw it glittering on the wall, and then the phantom appears on the lake during a full moon and everything.'

'So?'

'Well, it's funny we should see the second guinea glittering on Wariff Hill after we saw the phantom there . . . and during a full moon too.'

'That's just a coincidence,' I told him. 'It must be.'

'Still, it's odd isn't it?' said Totey.

Doubter agreed. 'The whole thing's odd. How come it was up at the fairy fort of all places that we saw the phantom *and* found the coin?'

'I can think of one reason,' said Cowlick. 'Old Daddy Armstrong said that's where the two lovers first met. So what could be more natural — or unnatural if you like — than that she should come back to haunt it?'

Doubter wasn't convinced. 'Maybe so, but what about the spade guinea? How did it get there?'

'That's what we've got to find out,' I said. 'Now I don't believe in ghosts . . .'

'Haw, haw, haw,' mocked the others in a loud chorus.

'All right, all right,' I said, 'maybe there *are* such things as ghosts, but I agree with Doubter. I never heard of a ghost that leaves golden guineas around or scribbles riddles on pieces of paper and wraps them around coins.'

'Maybe it was the running dead man,' suggested Totey.

'Don't be daft!' I said.

'What then?' asked Curly.

'I don't know — but who's game to find out?'

'What are you going to do?' asked Cowlick.

'See if the phantom appears at the same time tonight. And if it does — lie in wait for it up on the hill at the same time tomorrow night.'

After a bit of humming and hawing, the others agreed that that was the only way to get to the bottom of the affair and said they were game, which was just as well, because I wouldn't go up to Wariff Hill on my own in the daytime, let alone at night.

That evening we slipped out again, and from the stone bridge kept watch on the fairy fort. Sure enough, about the same time, we saw the strange ghostly light floating around the fort, just the way it had done the night before. Even though we were expecting it, it was all we could do not to run again, and next day our nerves were on edge at the very thought of going in under the hazels in the dark. Still, we said we'd go. We knew if we didn't we would never live it down, and once more we all slipped away under cover of darkness and met at the stone bridge.

It was a cloudy night, and now and then when the clouds covered the moon it was very dark. We decided that as this would make a walk across the fields difficult and dangerous — and it's a good distance from the bridge to Wariff Hill — to go up around by the Cottonbog Road instead. From there we could cut in by the edge of the bog and the swamps and go up by the only approach field, as Big Hughie always takes the bull in at night. So off we set, keeping close together and close by Prince.

A country road can be long and lonely when it's dark and there's not another sinner on it, and we were scared.

It wasn't so bad with Prince by our side. He'd take care
of anyone who would try and lay a hand on us. What did
scare us more than we cared to admit was what we couldn't
see. I had brought a torch with me, but the light it gave
only made the dark seem darker. As it was, the shadows
were dark and deep along the hedgerows and behind them,
and they seemed to be full of all sorts of unnatural rustlings
and whisperings. So much so, that before we knew it we
were casting sly glances from one side to the other, then
behind and then to the side again and in all the directions
in between, in case something might be creeping up on us.
Just what we were afraid might be creeping up on us we
didn't really know, but we couldn't help thinking about the
phantom and the running dead man and some of the other
scarey stories we had heard from Old Daddy Armstrong.

We remembered the story of the man who had been out
drinking and playing cards to all hours, and what had
happened to him on the way home. It was when he was
passing the graveyard that he saw it — a black pig running
along the top of the wall. Maybe Old Daddy Armstrong
didn't say so in so many words, but there was no doubting
what it was the man saw. It was the devil in pig's form.
That's why it was black.

More than once, I, for one, thought I saw something
black darting across the edge of a shadow. My heart pounded
and my throat dried up and I kept touching Prince's neck
with my fingers to make sure he was there. I knew the
others were thinking and seeing, or thinking they were seeing,
the same things, for all of a sudden we began to talk out
loud to give ourselves courage.

After a minute or two we recalled another story, the one
about the man who was walking along the road one night.
He heard footsteps behind him and when he looked around
he saw, coming after him, a pair of black shoes with nobody
in them — nobody he could see, that is — so he ran and

ran but the shoes kept running after him, and it wasn't until he turned in his own gate that they disappeared. We knew it was the devil again, following the man because he had been so bad, probably drinking and playing cards, like the man who saw the pig.

When we thought of the black shoes we stopped talking out loud and paused and listened, for we thought we heard a footstep behind us. But if there was anything, it stopped too. It was the same every time we walked on and stopped. So we started off faster than ever again, and soon we were walking so fast we were nearly running. Then the moon came out and lit up the road, and we could see there wasn't a thing on it except ourselves and the dog, so we slowed down.

A minute later the moon slid back behind the clouds, leaving the shadows deeper and darker than before, and soon we were thinking all sorts of weird things again. This time it wasn't about the black pig or the devil's shoes. It was about hearses and coffins, for it was on nights like this that the IRA gun-runners brought their hearses out. My father always told me about them whenever he got to talking about the Troubles.

The gun-runners would wait for a real dark night, and then they would set off with their hearses along the back roads. However, the police would be lying behind the hedges, waiting to stop the first hearse that came along, and when they did they would open the coffin to see if there really was a body in it, or, as they suspected, guns.

As we talked about it now, we could see it all, right down to the black top hats and the shining silver handles on the coffins. We could hear noises too. Nothing we could put our finger on, but they were there ... first behind one hedge, then another. Ahead a bit, then behind. They fitted just what we were thinking, and before we knew it, we were looking around again, expecting every minute to see figures flitting past or a gleaming black hearse gliding down the road behind us. It was so dark now we couldn't see as much as a coffin's length behind us. Yet we knew a hearse could go like the wind and just as quietly, and might be bearing down on us without us knowing it.

I took a good grip of Prince's collar and we skimmed along again for all we were worth and didn't slow down until we saw the glow of Gypsy Juno's fire up ahead. We felt a lot safer then.

We expected to hear Juno strumming on his guitar and maybe singing his favourite song, the one about the bridle hanging on the wall, but not so, and we soon found out why. He wasn't there. Rosie, his mother, was giving out for all she was worth. I couldn't repeat all she was saying, for her language was choice to say the least, but she was giving out about that good-for-nothing Juno going off and not bringing back as much as a bite to eat for his poor half-starved children. Probably drinking with that 'eejit' Shouting Sam again, she had no doubt, and knowing Juno as we did we felt she was more than likely right. When the dogs started barking we thought she was going to come out to see if there was any sign of him, so we slipped past as quickly as we could.

Shortly after that, the clouds broke up a bit and the moon came out for long spells and lit up the countryside, and we weren't as scared as when we set out. Soon Big Hughie's place was behind us, and we found the gate leading into the fields that border on the Cottonbog. The gate was partly open and we knew Big Hughie had taken the bull in for the night.

Wariff Hill looked darker and more sinister than ever now, but there was no turning back, and in we went. We kept well to the top of the fields so that we wouldn't stumble into the flax dams or the bog or the swamps, and felt our way cautiously along the hedges until we were at the foot of the field leading up to the hill. We scanned the fairy fort from the cover of the hedge. There was no light or movement on it as far as we could see, and on we pressed. Soon we were at the stone wall on the edge of the hazels. It looked terribly dark in below them, and I was glad I had brought my torch. Holding on to Prince and to each other, we started into the bushes.

If Wariff Hill is quiet in the day-time, it's quieter at night. Now and then we stopped and listened. There wasn't a stir. Our throats were dry and our eyes were like saucers as we tried to see through the wall of darkness beyond the yellow rim of torchlight.

Up and up we went, stumbling, stepping on each other's heels and toes, holding on, looking ahead, looking back, looking up and looking all around. At long last we saw the moonlight at the end of the tunnel of hazels. I switched off my torch and cautiously we crept forward the last few feet.

At the edge of the bushes we paused and scanned the fairy fort. Nothing moved. I licked my lips and still holding on to Prince, ventured out. The others followed, each holding on to the one in front. It was cold, but the sweat was breaking out on my brow. I looked at the moon; its face was leering down at us in a fearsome fashion.

Suddenly Prince gave a growl, and I could feel the hair rising on the back of his neck. The others felt me stiffen and we stopped in our tracks. Then we heard it, a long low groan that struck fear in our hearts. Where had it come from? What way could we run? For a moment we stood rooted to the spot. Terrifying thoughts flashed through my mind. I looked up at the fairy fort, half expecting to see the phantom rising up before us. There was nothing. The bull, I thought. I glanced around. Nothing. Then we heard it again. This time we didn't wait to see which way to run. We just ran.

We had hardly gone a few wild steps when we tripped and fell headlong. The groaning seemed right beneath us now, and our cries of fear added to the terror and confusion. Fortunately, as I picked myself up, I found my fingers slipping over something vaguely familiar, and as we raced for the hazels I realised what it was.

'Wait, wait!' I cried. 'That's Juno back there. It's Juno!'

I turned and picked my way back through the bracken with the aid of the torch and, sure enough, there was Juno lying on his back below a clump of ferns. Prince was licking his face, which we could see by the light of the torch was bruised and bleeding. He was only half conscious and couldn't talk. Gently we lifted him, Doubter and Curly taking his legs, Cowlick and myself his arms, and with Totey leading the way with the torch, we set out to carry him back to the caravan.

We never realised anyone could be so heavy. Juno was a dead weight and it was a nightmare carrying him down through the hazels and across the fields. After numerous trips, stumbles, and stops to rest, we finally reached the road. There we had another long rest before picking him up again and staggering the remaining half mile or so to the camp.

Rosie nearly threw a fit when she saw the state Juno was in, and so did his wife, but then, realising he wasn't drunk, they immediately started expressing the greatest concern for him and bathed his cuts and bruises with a tenderness we never dreamed they possessed. As a result, he had sufficiently recovered before we left to tell us what had happened, though not until he thanked us ten times over.

'B'dad, Tapser *alanna*,' he said, feeling the bruises on his puffed face, 'twas a good thing you recognised the feel of the badges on my belt. A good thing and no mistake.'

'Exposure you might have died from, Juno, exposure,' agreed his mother. 'And your poor face all cuts and bruises. What in the name of all that's holy happened? Sure I've never known you to take a fall like that, and you stone-cold sober.'

'A fall?' said Juno indignantly. 'A fall, was it?'

'You mean it wasn't a fall?' I asked him.

'Faith and it wasn't.' He groaned and lay back on the patchwork bedclothes while his mother and his wife took turns at holding a wet cloth to his forehead. We looked at each other and waited to hear.

'Yerra,' he said, 'I went up to the hill just before dark to check a few snares, and I was peeping down in through the briars at the first hole when two fellas stepped up behind me, caught me by the arms and spun me around ...'

'And then what?' asked Cowlick.

'Then,' he went on, 'this ignorant big culchie with the broken nose — a third one, mark you — stepped up and before I could say a word he starts beating the head off me.'

'Saints preserve us,' cried his mother, 'and what did he go and do a thing like that for?'

'That's what I'd like to know,' said Juno angrily. 'I wouldn't mind, but there I was, not able to lift a hand to defend myself, and him twice as big. Oh, if only I could have got my hands on him, just once.'

'What happened after that?' asked Doubter.

'That's the last I remember. They must have beaten me unconscious. The next thing I knew I was here, thanks to you lads.'

'But why should anyone want to beat *you* up?' asked Curly.

'And him not interfering with anybody,' asserted his wife.

Except, of course, that he was snaring rabbits, I thought, but that was no reason why anyone should beat him up.

Juno shook his head, wincing with the pain. 'I don't know ... I just don't know.'

'I know,' piped up Totey.

We all looked at him.

'Well, they must have wanted to rob you, Juno! Look ... why else would they turn your pockets inside-out?'

'Begorra, you're right,' said Juno, sitting up and holding out the lining of his pockets. 'Now isn't that the strangest thing?'

Indeed it was, as we all agreed on our way home. Why should anyone want to rob Juno? Everyone knows he has nothing worth stealing, and certainly not money.

8. LOST IN THE NIGHT

Next day we went up to the plantation in the hope that Old Daddy Armstrong might have had another visit from Felicity. We were in luck. She had dropped by the day before and he had some very interesting news for us. He said that when he told her about the missing bracelet being in the photograph taken *after* her fall in the plantation, she got as flustered as a clocking hen. She apologised for the trouble she had put us to, said she must have made a mistake about when she lost it, and explained that with things the way they were at the castle she didn't know whether she was coming or going.

'What did she mean by that?' I asked him.

'Well,' he said, 'it seems there's something a mite strange going on over there. For one thing, the place is in a jitter over weird noises that have been besetting the castle in the dead of night. The staff are scared stiff. According to Felicity they're convinced that the knocking and rattling they've been hearing can be nothing but the ghost of the running dead

man, and they're all for packing up and leaving. Then there's
her father.'

'What about her father?' asked Cowlick.

'It appears from what she tells me that the Major's gone
a bit peculiar,' and the old man tapped his head to emphasise
the point. 'She's worried about him. Says he's acting very
strange these days, muttering to himself, locking himself
in his room for hours on end, and wandering through the
trees as if he's gone out of his head.'

We looked at each other knowingly.

'And that's not all,' said Old Daddy Armstrong. 'Some
nights ago young Mr. Rochford-King heard something in
the library — apparently they haven't been able to pinpoint
the other noises — so he rushed down. The library, she
says, is directly below his bedroom. Major Boucher, it seems,
had heard it too and was there before him. They found
that somebody had been at one of those valuable paintings
I was telling you about. Felicity's father was straightening
it up when Mr. Rochford-King arrived, because it was
hanging sideways as if somebody had tried to take it down.

'A nearby window was open too, and Felicity thinks a
gang of crooks maybe read about the paintings in the
newspaper article I showed you, and were trying to steal
them. The police were called, and now they're wiring every
inch of the estate wall so that nobody can get in without
setting off the alarm.'

We thanked him and left. We were buzzing with
excitement after what he had told us. We felt a bit guilty
about not telling him of our own experiences, but we felt
we couldn't, at least not yet — not until we had a better
idea of what was going on. We also knew that if what we
had discovered got back to the castle, or if it got around
to the wrong ears, we might never get the chance to find
out what it was all about. Just what the goings-on at Wariff
Hill had to do with the goings-on at the castle we couldn't

imagine, but we were convinced that all these strange happenings were part of the same thing. The problem was we couldn't get into the castle now because of the new burglar alarm. That left only one course open to us. We would have to make another visit to Wariff Hill, and we decided to go that night.

As the day wore on, the weather closed in in a most unexpected way. The sky clouded over low and it got very warm; not pleasantly warm but uncomfortably warm and close, and there wasn't a breath of wind. My father said it looked as if a storm was brewing, and he wouldn't be surprised if it was a thunderstorm, judging by the heat. My father can read the weather as well as he can read a rabbit–burrow, and I just hoped the storm would hold off long enough for us to get to Wariff Hill and back.

By tea-time the storm was still hanging, although a slight drizzle had started. We all went to bed early, as arranged, using the rain as an excuse so as not to arouse the suspicion of our folks. Then we slipped out before dark and cut across the fields. The grass was wet, but we had taken good care to wear our Wellingtons.

We were just going down to the ruined farmhouse by the flax dams when we spotted Big Hughie and two other men walking a little way ahead of us. I shouted a greeting to him, and what a surprise I got! Obviously startled, the men turned around. The tall one wasn't Big Hughie at all but a man with a broken nose, and in that instant we realised they could be none other than the three scoundrels who had beaten up poor Juno. Before we could move another step, they clambered through the hedge at the side of the ruins, and when we got to the spot, Prince, who had rushed forward, was standing on top of the ditch barking after them as they disappeared into the gathering gloom.

We were excited, if just a bit frightened, and after a brief halt to recover our composure, we decided to go on. First though, we searched around for a good heavy stick each. Armed with them, and the knowledge that with Prince by our side we could give a good account of ourselves against anything human, we set off again at a good pace so that we could reach the fairy fort before it was completely dark.

Lighted windows twinkling in the castle away below were the only signs of life we could see from the top of Wariff Hill as we scanned the darkening countryside. We decided to make one quick search of the area around the fort before concealing ourselves among the hazels. As we split up, we agreed that if any of us found anything or ran into any trouble, we would give three blasts on our bourtree whistle. Nobody did, and after a minute or two we were slipping back, one by one, to a pre-arranged spot beneath the hazels on the edge of the clearing.

Soon we were all there, except Cowlick. Anxiously we awaited his return. Prince shook the rain from his coat. The minutes ticked by. We gripped our sticks and strained our eyes to try and pierce the darkness. Still there was no sign of Cowlick. Unable to contain my anxiety another minute I switched on my torch, blew three times on my bourtree whistle and waited for the answering call. It never came.

9. THE STORM BREAKS

It's difficult to describe the way we felt as we waited there beneath the dripping hazels, trying desperately to see through the darkness and the drizzle for any sign of Cowlick.

If you've ever been poaching and waited in vain for a ferret to come out of a rabbit-warren, you'll know how we felt. There comes a moment when you know the ferret should be coming out, and isn't. Then there comes another moment when you realise that no amount of coaxing is going to bring it out. You can't see it but you know something has gone wrong, and you know you'll be lucky if you ever see it again. There's nothing you can do about it, except wait, and you know that if you do wait there's the danger you'll be caught.

That's the way it was with us up at the fairy fort. If we were scared before, we were in a right panic now. When the bleeps of the bourtree whistle had died away in the darkness, an awful silence fell, and even though it was wet we were so warm we were sweating, and we were trying so hard to see something that it wasn't long before we were seeing all sorts of things. Somehow there seemed to be movements in the shadows, and after the way Cowlick had disappeared I knew it could only be one thing — fairies or leprechauns creeping through the darkness towards us — and I could imagine the phantom about to rise up out of the fairy fort to urge them on to claim us too.

The others, I could feel, were full to choking with the same fearful thoughts, and in the end, I'm afraid, we turned and ran, and we didn't stop until we reached the Cottonbog Road. There we huddled behind the hedge and looked back. The hill was a scraggy shadow looming up into the warm, wet night, and we became more than ever aware of the oppressive heat and the eerie atmosphere all around us as we watched ... for what we did not know. Nothing stirred to break the stillness, and we wondered what we would do.

Some of the boys thought we should slip back down home and say nothing about Cowlick's disappearance. I didn't think so. I knew that if we were all at home in the morning and Cowlick wasn't, questions would be asked. The cat would soon be out of the bag, and there would be such a hullabaloo we wouldn't be allowed outside the house again.

On the other hand, if none of us was there, our folks might think we had all slipped out early in the morning and maybe not worry too much about it, at least for the day. In the meantime, I told the others, we could sleep in one of Big Hughie's cowsheds on the edge of the Cottonbog, and in the morning go back to Wariff Hill and have a good look for Cowlick.

The boys weren't too sure of my idea at first, but when they thought about it they realised we couldn't go home without Cowlick. They also knew we couldn't stay in the open much longer. If the heat meant thunder, it also meant lightning, and none of us likes to be out in the open when there's lightning, especially when we're wet and everything else is wet. So in the end, with a last anxious and guilty glance back up at the sinister shadow which we had been forced to leave without Cowlick, we crossed into the fields on the other side of the road and made our way along the bog towards the cowsheds.

We had decided on the second cowshed, as the first one is open at both ends, but the first one had quite a surprise in store for us. We were about a field's length from it when we saw a flickering light in it. Our first instinct was to run. Then we realised the light was from an open fire, and we were immediately curious. Holding on to Prince, I led the way forward.

As we stole closer we could see shadows in the firelight, and even before we saw their faces we recognised the voices of none other than Juno and Shouting Sam. They were sitting on stones by the side of the fire, and now and then they would take a swig from a bottle or turn a rabbit cooking on a spit.

'You know what, Shuno,' we heard Shouting Sam say drunkenly, 'I think it wash shusht a — hic — shusht a ghosht!'

'A ghosht, a ghosht was it?' repeated Juno, and bending closer to Sam, he pointed to his own forehead with the bottle and asked, 'Does that look like a ghosht? Huh — huh?'

Shouting Sam blinked hard as he tried to focus on the bruises Juno was showing him.

Juno looked at him. 'Ah!' he exclaimed, taking another swig of the bottle and wiping his mouth with his sleeve, 'you know what I think? I think you're drunk — drunk ash a, ash a . . .'

He seemed to be so full of drink himself that it was lapping up around his throat, and he swallowed hard to keep it down.

We moved closer, excited by what Shouting Sam had

said. Was this mention of a ghost just drunken talk? Or
had he seen something on Wariff Hill too? We didn't want
to delay in case they might spot us. Yet we thought that
if we waited just a little longer we might learn something.

Prince had other ideas. Before we could stop him, he
struggled free and streaked towards the fire. With a fierce
snarl and a flash of fangs, he hurled himself straight at them,
right up over the fire. The sight of that powerful black form
leaping from the shadows must have struck terror into their
hearts. Picking themselves up, they fled screaming into the
darkness beyond, the loud-speaker and all the other
paraphernalia that Sam always carries around with him
banging loudly as they ran.

Minutes later we could still hear them crashing through
the hedges and ditches and we guessed they wouldn't stop
until they reached the Cottonbog Road.

At a loss to understand what had got into Prince, we
ran forward. He came back into the light of the fire, and
when we saw what it was, we had to laugh. It wasn't Juno
and Shouting Sam he had gone for at all. It was the rabbit
cooking on the spit! He had got it too, spit and all, in that
powerful leap across the fire.

Poor Prince, he must have been starving when he got
the smell of that rabbit. It *did* smell appetising. Suddenly
we realised we were as hungry as he was, and that he would
have to share it. Quickly we retrieved a good portion of
it that he hadn't touched and tucked in, taking the precaution
at the same time of keeping enough for another meal.

We wondered where Juno and Sam had stopped running,
and it occurred to us that with all the drink they had taken
they might pluck up enough courage to sneak back. If so,
the sooner we moved on to the other cowshed, the better.
Before leaving, we took the stones that ringed the fire and
rolled them over into the nearest hedge and put out the
fire and scattered the ashes. Thus, we thought, if they did

venture back, they'd find no trace of the fire in the darkness and might think in their drunkenness they had imagined the whole thing.

There were several cows in the other shed. We could see them in the light of the torch, lying together on the earthen floor, as we climbed the rickety stairs to the loft. Our outside clothes were soaked, so we took them off, together with our Wellingtons and socks, and left them on a bale of straw to dry. Then we snuggled down into the hay.

As the rain dripped down the worn timbers and the cows chewed peacefully on their cuds below, we pondered over the mysterious disappearance of Cowlick.

'He can't have vanished into thin air,' I said.

'Maybe he couldn't find us in the dark and went on home,' suggested Doubter from the darkness on my left.

'But all he had to do was blow his bourtree whistle,' I said.

'Or give us a shout,' added Curly.

'Unless he got further away than he thought,' said Doubter, 'and he didn't hear us and we didn't hear him.'

'. . . and lost his way and is scared to move for fear he might walk into the swamps,' put in Totey.

'I don't know,' I said. 'It's all very strange. Still, I hope you're right. If so, he'll be sheltering round about somewhere. Maybe he's even found a cowshed, too, on the edge of the hazels. Anyway, we'll go back and look for him in the morning.'

'Seeing as we haven't found any phantom, what do you think is going on up on Wariff Hill?' asked Doubter.

'Yes,' said Curly, 'if it wasn't the phantom, what *was* the ghostly light we saw? And what has it got to do with the legend?'

'Maybe somebody's watching the castle from up there,' suggested Totey.

'In the dark?' said I. 'Don't forget it's at night these things seem to happen on Wariff Hill.'

'Maybe,' said Curly, 'somebody's practising black magic up there at night — to try and solve the legend.' There was no comment, and he went on. 'Why not? Weren't places like that used for human sacrifices and all sorts of things long ago?'

'Maybe so,' I said, 'but I'm beginning to think it's nothing so far-fetched as phantoms and black magic. Did it ever occur to you that maybe somebody is using the hill to signal somebody at the castle?'

'You mean Felicity's father, or some of the ex-convicts?' suggested Doubter.

'What for?' asked Curly.

'I don't know,' I said, 'but you must admit, it might explain the light we've been seeing up there.'

Just then the storm broke, and even though we had been expecting it all evening, it broke with such suddenness it gave us a start. The first flash lit up the whole loft through a small netting-wire window near the roof. Seconds later, an ear-splitting burst of thunder erupted right over the shed and rolled away across the Cottonbog. After that there was dead silence, but only for a moment or too. Suddenly the heavens opened, and the rain came thundering down in torrents.

That was the start of it. The rain settled down to a steady downpour, and flashes of lightning and thunder continued at intervals, and we were glad we were inside and not out in it. We are scared of any kind of lightning, but flash lightning scares us more than the forked kind. Flash lightning seems to run across the ground and flit over everything and we've never liked the idea of being out in the open and in the way of it. It's always a sickening flash too, like the yellow-blue light that comes from the electric wires when high winds make them touch.

After a real bright flash we would wait for the thunder, knowing that when the lightning was bright the thunder would be very loud, and when it would go ripping across the shed we would try and imagine what it was. Somehow we couldn't get away from the idea that it was caused by big black clouds crashing together like giant boulders. It was powerful and frightening at the same time, and we snuggled still farther into the hay and tried to guess where and when the next clap would come, and we listened to the rain drumming on the felt roof.

Normally, I think, there's nothing nicer than to be warm and comfortable and to be lying listening to the rain, but there was nothing nice about it that night. We were thinking of it falling in sheets on the hazel-bushes that cover Wariff Hill. We were thinking of Cowlick somewhere in among them, enveloped by the darkness and the storm, a victim of the Legend of the Golden Key.

I for one couldn't help thinking of that part of the legend that goes:

> *The man is dead*
> *But life allows*
> *He'll run forever*
> *Beneath the boughs. . .*

I couldn't help wondering if Cowlick was thinking about it up there in the hazels, or wherever he was. Indeed, wherever he was, for where could he be? What could have befallen him? I closed my eyes. Eventually the thunder shifted away from the Cottonbog, and we dropped off into a troubled sleep.

10. UNVEILING THE MISTS

The chittering of goldfinches woke us next morning. Prince was already awake and licking himself down, and the cows had gone out to graze. It was a lovely day. The clouds were white, there was plenty of blue sky and the sun was already drying out the storm-washed fields. The Cottonbog was sparkling with tufts of cotton-grass and soft stars of thistledown, barely dry, drifted across the fields.

There was nobody about, and without further ado we cut back across the road to Wariff Hill. The bull wasn't in the field, which was lucky for us, as the swamps were flooded from the night's rain. Taking good care to stay together, we searched the hill and the fairy fort. We were hoping against hope that we would find Cowlick sheltering under a bush or behind a boulder. Desperately we searched and searched. We looked everywhere, but there was no sign of him. Finally, feeling utterly disheartened and full of fresh fears for his safety, we returned to the hide-out.

We were hungry and dirty, so we scouted around until

we found a spring of nice clear water and had a long drink
and freshened up. We also found water-cress, and picked
a handful of the best and washed it. Then we made our
way up to a large patch of thistles and ragwort at the top
of the field, and hunkered down in the middle of it. In
there nobody could see us, and we could keep an eye on
Wariff Hill and the road, as well as the fields right back
to Big Hughie's place and to the castle. While the goldfinches
had their breakfast on the thistle-tops, we finished off the
remainder of the rabbit. It tasted good with the water-cress
and we made the best of it, as we knew it might be a long
time before we got anything more to eat.

After that we began talking things over and planning our
next move. The question was, what had happened to
Cowlick? Where was he? Had he lost his way and walked
into the swamps, or had he stumbled into the hands of
whatever or whoever was behind the strange goings-on at
Wariff Hill? Surely, we reasoned, he knew only too well
the danger of the swamps, especially in the darkness, and
would have been extra careful to avoid them. No, whatever
had happened to him must have happened quickly — so
quickly that he hadn't been able to shout or sound a warning
bleep on his bourtree whistle. Had he been seized by someone
spying on the castle — perhaps the broken-nosed man and
his companions? If so, why? And who were they?

Or had something even more sinister befallen him? What
did it all have to do with the Legend of the Golden Key,
the phantom, and the lost treasure of the Kings, or with
the attempt to steal the paintings?

We had a lot of questions, and few answers. Then, as
we pondered them and had another look at the spade guinea
we had found, something Curly had said gave me an idea.
It was what he had said about black magic. Wasn't Juno
always offering to get his mother to tell us our fortune?
Wasn't he always saying how she possessed the power to

'penetrate the mysterious mists of time that veil the future', to use his own words? Maybe she could use her strange powers to enlighten us on the events that had resulted in Cowlick's disappearance. Maybe even tell us where he was.

Being at a loss to know what to do, and unable to make a better suggestion, the others agreed that at least it was worth a try, so off we set. We crossed the road and headed along the fields towards Juno's camp. On the way we spotted him on the roadside supervising the usual hive of activity that surrounds road-making operations. Curious, we stole up behind a hedge to have a closer look. My father and Doubter's father were there, as they work for the council, and we were relieved to see them, for it meant our absence from home hadn't been noticed yet. We could also see that one of Juno's carts was leaning sideways on a broken wheel near a large hole in the road. It looked as if it had come a cropper in a cave-in caused by the night's heavy rain. True to form, Juno was making a big thing of it, saying he couldn't understand it and how he might have been killed and a lot of balderdash like that. Of course, he was enjoying every minute of it. We didn't like the idea of approaching Rosie direct, but we knew Juno would be there all day, so we decided to go ahead and chance finding her in an agreeable mood.

Whether it was because we had carried Juno home from Wariff Hill or not, I don't know, but Rosie actually invited us in. Normally we wouldn't have ventured into the caravan with her for love or money. Her bulging eyes, her long nose and her straggly hair make her look like — well, like a witch. On this occasion, however, we were in no position to be fussy about a thing like that, and in no time at all we were sitting staring at that glass ball of hers. We told her everything, except about the spade guinea, in case she might want it as payment, and asked her if she could please tell us where our friend Cowlick was.

Round and round the crystal ball Rosie wove her scrawny hands, at the same time saying all sorts of gibberish we couldn't understand. All the while her eyes were getting bigger. Finally, speaking as if she was in a trance and seeing it all in the depths of the crystal ball, she told us,

> *Your friend is well*
> *But for how long*
> *I cannot tell*
> *My ball is dark*
> *With some bad deed*
> *Of this my sign*
> *You must take heed*
> *In timeless mists*
> *A glitter I behold*
> *What could it be*
> *Could it be . . . gold?*

We looked at each other, and she continued,

> *One is tall, one is fair*
> *That this foul deed*
> *It would ensnare . . .*

'But, but . . .' I started. But before I could ask her anything she was on her feet, and with a sweep of her hand bade us,

> *Go, make haste*
> *Bid them beware . . .*

One thing for certain, we made haste out of that caravan and back up to the hide-out. If we ever doubted Rosie's ability to tell fortunes, we didn't doubt it now. We could hardly think, we were so excited. She hadn't told us where Cowlick was, but she did say he was well. Also, we knew now that the time had come when we must warn the Kings that there was a plot to steal not only their paintings but, we believed, the lost treasure of the Legend of the Golden Key which they needed so much. We must tell them all we knew, help them expose the thieves and, we could only hope, find Cowlick in the process.

The problem was, how to get to the castle. If we went home, the police would be brought in to search for Cowlick and there would be such a commotion that whoever was after the treasure would be put on their guard and might never be flushed out. If we walked straight up to the lodge gate of the castle, the chances were that we wouldn't be allowed in. At the same time we couldn't get in over the wall now, if it was being fitted with a burglar alarm as Old Daddy Armstrong had said.

For a long while it seemed to us there was nothing we could do.

'Unless we could wade in under the bridge,' suggested Curly.

Doubter shook his head. 'The river would be too deep now with all the rain.'

'That's true,' I said. 'But wait . . . wait! Maybe we could build some sort of raft that would take us under the bridge.'

'That's it,' Curly agreed, 'a raft.'

'But we couldn't make a raft over there,' said Doubter. 'Somebody in the estate would be sure to spot us, and we could never carry it over that far.'

'We wouldn't have to do either,' I explained. 'Isn't the river in flood? We could build it at the back of the Whin Hill where nobody would see us, and sail down the river.'

'Okay,' said Doubter, 'but what will we make it with?'

'There's a coil of rope here in the cowshed,' I said. 'Let's get it and come on. I've an idea.'

It was lunch-time, and the scene of the road-making operations was deserted. Having made sure no one was watching, we took an empty tar barrel each and rolled them down to the wooden bridge on the edge of Mr. Stockman's corn fields. Then I despatched Doubter to get a good long ash pole for pushing the raft, while Curly, Totey and I made our way back up the fields to the wooden gate that leads out on to the brae. Sensing something was afoot, Prince was as excited as could be.

'What do you think you're doing?' asked Curly when I started to uncoil the wire that held the gate in place.

'I'm taking off the gate. Come on, give me a hand.'

'Mr. Stockman will have your life,' protested Curly. 'And anyway, what's the big idea?'

'Simple!' I said. 'We tie the barrels under the gate ... and we have a raft.'

'But you can't go and take a man's gate just like that,' said Curly.

'Why not?' I said. 'We'll only be doing him a favour. The corn is nearly ripe, and he'll be taking the gate off soon himself to let in the combine harvester. Anyhow, this is a desperate situation and it requires desperate measures. Cowlick would do the same for you, wouldn't he?'

Curly couldn't argue with that, so he pitched in and gave a hand, while Totey kept watch to make sure we weren't caught in the act.

Doubter, who was waiting at the wooden bridge, nearly threw a fit when he saw the gate, but I soon persuaded him of the sense in taking it. In no time at all, the raft was ready, and having anchored it to the bridge with a piece of left-over rope, we gathered round and lifted it into the water. Immediately it was caught in the brown, swiftly flowing floodwater, the mooring rope sprang taut, and to our delight it bobbed buoyantly a few yards down the bank.

It seemed for one awful moment, however, that our plan was doomed to failure before it began. Just as we were boarding the raft, an angry shout rang out from the Whin Hill.

'It's Mr. Stockman!' cried Doubter.

'What's he shouting about?' I asked.

'I don't know,' said Curly. 'But he seems very annoyed at something.'

'Crikey, look!' yelled Totey, and turning around we followed his pointing finger. Our hearts sank at what we saw.

'It's Juno's horses,' cried Doubter. 'They're in the corn. What are we going to do?'

'There's only one thing we can do,' I yelled. 'Cast off, Doubter, cast off!'

For once Doubter didn't hesitate. Untying the rope, he raced back to the raft as Curly held it steady with the steering pole. Willing hands hauled him aboard, Curly withdrew the pole, and we were away.

11. VOYAGE TO DANGER

The current had taken us about two hundred yards from the bridge when Mr. Stockman came running down to it. As always when he's working, the hardy little white-haired farmer had his shirt sleeves rolled up and the neck wide open. He paused on the middle of the bridge and brandishing a fist, yelled at us, 'Hey! Did you boys open that gate up there?'

The only answer he got was a bark from Prince, who was standing with this front paws on the end bar of the raft looking back.

Crossing over, Mr. Stockman appeared for a moment as if he was going to come after us. He hesitated. We could see he was trying to make up his mind whether to chase us or the horses. In the end, he decided on the horses and with a bellow of, 'Bad luck to you!' turned and ran towards the top of the field where Juno's horses were in the corn.

On board the raft we breathed a sigh of relief, although we still felt a bit shaken by what had happened.

'Wait until he finds out we took the gate,' said Doubter.

'He'll really be hopping mad,' said Curly.

'How was I to know Juno's horses would come in?' I asked irritably. 'I thought I was doing him a good turn taking down the gate.'

Curly shook his head. 'He'll never believe it.'

'He'll have to,' I said. 'Anyway, we can worry about that when the time comes. We've more important things to worry about now.'

Wielding the ash pole with growing skill, Curly steered the raft down the middle of the swollen river. Slowly the sounds from the farmyard faded, leaving a glorious peace that was broken only by the chirping of the birds and the occasional cry of a startled water-hen as it rose from the rushes and flew ahead, its long feet trailing the water. Our thoughts, however, were as dark and as troubled as the muddy currents beneath us. Cowlick was constantly in our minds, and fears for his safety kept flooding into a jumble of thoughts of treasure and of the many things we couldn't explain.

Almost before we knew it, we came to a bend where the river is wide and rocky. In spite of the rain the rocks were still visible, and we knew we were going to have a rough passage. With eyes glued on the first of them, we held Prince and braced ourselves. We hit it with a jarring boom that sent a shudder through all four barrels. The raft slewed from side to side in a crazy zig-zag as it bounced from one to another, and we held on tightly until at last it came to a halt, the left side tilted in the air, the other buried in the rushing water.

'I thought we were all in for a ducking there,' gasped Curly as we scrambled up the dry side of the raft.

'I very nearly went in,' said Doubter.

'Me too,' said Curly. 'The jolt almost knocked the pole out of my hands.'

'Did you hear the boom, boom, boom?' asked Totey.

'We hit the rocks hard, all right,' I said. 'I wonder if it did any damage?'

Cautiously shifting our weight, we examined the ends of the barrels that were sticking up out of the water. There were a few big dents in them, but as far as we could see, none of them had been holed.

'I think we're okay,' I said, 'but we're going to have a job getting over these rocks. Come on. There's only one way to do it.'

Fortunately we had ended up on rocks not far from the bank, where the water wasn't too deep. Leaving Totey on board to hold Prince and our Wellingtons, we dropped over the side, and with the water gushing around us began heaving the raft over the rocks. It was an awkward job, and once Doubter nearly disappeared into a hole, but we perservered and eventually got the raft over into deeper water.

Soon we were sailing along nicely again, past the alders and the otter pool, round the back of Wariff Hill and through the Cottonbog.

Everything went well until we came to where our river joins the main river that flows into the estate. All of a sudden we found ourselves going too fast. Because of the rain, the flow of our river as it was sucked into the other one was much greater than we had expected. Again we realised there was nothing we could do except hold on and hope for the best.

With Prince firmly wedged between my knees, we gripped the edge of the raft and held on for dear life. We were at the mercy of the current as it swept us out into the mainstream. The raft spun around, dipped dangerously in the swirling water and shot towards the far bank at a dizzy speed. Somehow we held on. Boom! We rebounded with a bang and spun out into the middle of the river, there to resume a nice smooth course to our great relief.

Our relief, however, was short-lived. We discovered to our horror that all four of us were not, in fact, on board! Totey was missing, and there was no sign of him in the dark rushing water.

'Pull in, pull in,' I cried.

Curly responded immediately, plunging the pole into the bottom and throwing his full weight on to it. However, he hadn't reckoned on the faster flowing current and the muddy bed of the river. The pole stuck fast, the raft drew away, and for one terrifying moment he found himself stretched between the two. Then, to the utter amazement of everyone, including himself, he was left high and dry, clinging to the pole in mid-river!

I realised there was only one thing to do. We were a good few feet from the bank, and we could never jump it. Instead, I lifted Prince and lobbed him as far as I could. He swam ashore and shook himself.

'Quick, Prince, catch,' I yelled, and hurled the mooring rope towards him. He snapped, and missed, but flung himself after the end of the rope as it snaked away through the grass, and caught it. The raft immediately swung into the bank, and Doubter and I jumped ashore.

Curly was shouting for help, and his plight would have been funny if it hadn't been so serious. He couldn't hold on for long, and if he fell in we knew he would drown as he couldn't swim. We had to get to him and fast.

'We must get the raft out to him,' I cried to Doubter. 'Come on! Give me a hand.'

Grabbing the rope, we began dragging the raft back up the river. It was a heavy pull against the current, and the raft kept jamming against the bank. To add to the confusion, Prince was running up and down, barking loudly.

'Hurry,' yelled Curly. 'Hurry, for goodness sake. The pole's staring to slip.'

'Okay, hold on a minute,' I shouted.

We had the raft almost opposite him now, but we needed it above him. There was no time to lose; the pole was slipping and he was hanging dangerously close to the water.

'Right,' I told Doubter, 'that's far enough. Hold it until I get on. Now, give a good shove.'

Still holding on to the rope, Doubter put his foot to the side of the raft and shoved as hard as he could. The raft shot out into the middle of the river, the current caught it and swept it down towards Curly. Doubter, however, had shoved the raft too hard. It was now heading straight for the pole. If it hit it, Curly would be knocked into the water. Fortunately, Doubter realised this too. He pulled on the rope. The raft narrowly missed the pole and sailed directly under Curly. I quickly pulled him aboard, and the pole came away quite easily with him.

On reaching the bank, Curly threw his arms around Prince and hugged him gratefully. 'Boy, I thought I was done for there,' he gasped.

'You would have been, too, if it hadn't been for Prince,' I said, giving him a well-earned pat. 'Are you all right?'

Curly swallowed hard and nodded, then sat up with a jerk. 'What about Totey?'

In our panic we had forgotten all about poor Totey!

'What about Totey?' asked a familiar voice.

We swung around, and once again gave a huge sigh of relief. There, walking down the bank towards us, his hands in his pockets and a wide grin on his freckled face, was none other than Totey himself. He wasn't even wet. Eagerly we gathered around him to find out what had happened. It had been something very simple really. When the raft hit the bank, Totey had lost his grip and was catapulted over into the field.

'So that's where you went?' I smiled, giving him a friendly wigging. 'We thought for a minute there you had been drowned.'

We sat down to get our breath back and plan our next move.

'What now?' Doubter asked me.

'I say we press on. The sooner we get to the estate the better, okay?'

In spite of the frightening experiences we had just been through, all three of them nodded.

'Right,' I said. 'Now the chances are that we'll have to hide out in the estate for some time, and we have to eat. So, Doubter, you take a turn at the pole. Curly and I will put out a line and see what we can catch.'

We boarded the raft, and set sail once more.

Almost before we knew it, we had gone under the bridge on the boundary of the estate and were gliding quietly through the heavily wooded grounds. It was warm and sunny and very peaceful. On either side of us the sun sparkled on leathery rhododendron leaves, and the only sounds were the gurgling of the water and the cawing of rooks high in the trees. Somehow, phantoms and plots and treasure all seemed very unreal in such a peaceful setting. Yet nothing could be more real than the cold hard fact that Cowlick had disappeared, or the solid gold guinea which I fingered thoughtfully in my trousers pocket.

Knowing that Mr. Moxley, the gamekeeper, and his son Dan would be patrolling the estate more than ever now after the attempt to steal the paintings, we talked in whispers and then only when necessary, and kept a close watch on both banks of the river. We saw no one and, we felt sure, no one saw us as we sailed out into the lake. The only movement came from a small wooded island in the middle of the lake. Birds of all kinds were fluttering around its closely knit tree-tops, and swans and ducks and seagulls were swimming around its shores. Otherwise we had the lake to ourselves as we floated not far from the bank. It was plain sailing now — or so we thought. How were we to know that at that very moment we were sailing into the greatest danger.

An excited bark from Prince and a shout from Totey switched our attention from the island to the left side of the raft.

'There's something on the line,' Totey was saying. 'Look, there it goes again.'

So there was, and what a surprise! Our makeshift line had been farthest from our thoughts. Now it was as tight as a bow-string and slicing the water like a knife. Bending down, and at the same time holding on to me to keep from falling in, Doubter reached out, twirled it around his forefinger, and slowly drew it towards him.

Whatever was on the end of the line was well and truly hooked. As my father always says, 'You can't beat a worm for bait when a river's in flood.'

'Boy, it must be a big one,' said Doubter.

'Is it a trout?' Totey asked him.

'I don't know,' he replied, 'but it's a big one, whatever it is.'

'Maybe it's a salmon,' said Curly.

'It's hardly a salmon,' I said, 'or it would be away with the line like a shot.'

'What is it, then?' asked Totey.

'Could be just an eel,' I said. 'You know the way they curl around a line. You'd think you'd hooked the Loch Ness monster.'

'Crikey, it must be a big one all right,' gasped Totey. 'Look, it's pulling the raft!'

We looked around in disbelief, but we knew at once there was something in what he had said. The bank had slipped away behind us. We were moving all right — and in the wrong direction!

I swung around. 'It's not the fish that's pulling us!'

'What then?' asked Curly.

'Listen, can you not hear it?'

'The Devil's Cup!' cried Doubter.

I bit my lip. 'It's the Cup all right. The water's flowing into it — and it's pulling us with it. . .'

There was a horrified silence. We had completely forgotten about the Devil's Cup. Now we realised that with all the heavy rain and the river in flood, much more water than usual was spilling over into it, setting up a powerful current all around.

'Quick, Curly,' I shouted. 'Try and swing us clear of the current.'

Curly, who had been holding the pole for Doubter, immediately, but with more caution than the last time, plunged it into the water. Instead of sticking to the bottom, however, the pole disappeared, only to bob up again a yard or two away. 'It's too deep,' he cried. 'It's too deep.'

Prince, who was standing on the front of the raft looking towards the Devil's Cup, was barking loudly, and we could see he sensed the danger it held for us.

'Maybe Prince can do it again,' suggested Doubter.

'We're too far from the bank,' I said, 'but he might be able to swim for help if we could throw him clear of the current.' Calling the collie to the back of the raft, I pointed to the bank and urged him, 'Go seek'm, boy, seek'm.' Doubter gave me a hand, and we swung him in towards the shore as far as we could. Up he popped, paddled round once in a small circle, and made a beeline for dry land. Anxiously we watched him scramble out, but instead of racing for help, he shook the water from his coat and stood barking at us. Our hearts sank, and we were left with a feeling as empty as the Cup itself.

'What are we going to do now?' cried Totey. 'We're going to be drowned. We're all going to be drowned.'

I tried to reassure him. 'Nobody's going to be drowned. Not if we keep our heads. We'll get out of this — somehow.'

However, he continued to cry. I couldn't fool him any more than I could fool Doubter or Curly, or for that matter myself. Slowly, but surely, we were being drawn closer and closer to that awful Cup. The roar of water as it plunged fifty feet or more to the bottom was growing louder and louder. We could see no way of escape. The only outlet was the narrow tunnel at the bottom of the giant bowl which carried the water away beneath the estate to goodness knows where. Some people said it came out under the boating lake, but no one was sure if it ever came out anywhere. One thing was certain; nothing could survive being swept down it. And on the far side of the Cup rose the spike-topped wall which we could never hope to climb, even if we could reach it. We were trapped.

Grimly we gripped the edge of the raft, our eyes rivetted on that gaping hole that was swallowing up the lake. We couldn't take our eyes off it, and you may not believe this but I could swear that as we watched mesmerised we could see in the cloud of spray that hung over the cup, a form — the white wispy form of that poor girl Old Daddy Armstrong was telling us about ... a pale pathetic figure, her long silken hair rising and falling around her shoulders, a slender hand outstretched towards us ... beckoning us ... luring us ever closer to the doom that had been hers so many years before ...

As we were sucked towards the boiling cauldron we could see that wispy form of the girl as plainly as anything ... one minute. Next minute, when I wrenched my eyes away and told the boys to snap out of it, she vanished in a wafting sort of way among the millions of tiny floating drops of water, so that we wondered if what we had seen really was her at all, or just the rising clouds of white spray.

Totey was sobbing. The other two, faces deathly pale, looked at me as if my voice had come from far away. What could I do? I had never felt so helpless in all my life. Yet I knew I must do something. Anything! In desperation I threw another frightened glance at the Devil's Cup, and spotted something on the rim of it — two iron spikes about a yard apart and jutting about a foot above the water. In those two spikes I suddenly saw a chance of survival. A slim chance, but there was no other.

'Quickly,' I yelled above the roar of the water. 'Steer for those spikes. Use your hands and steer for those spikes.'

That snapped Curly and Doubter out of their trance and they began splashing with their hands for dear life. At the same time I threw myself downwards at the front of the raft, and reaching into the water unscrewed the bung from the first barrel. Almost immediately the barrel began filling up, and the nose of the raft dipped lower and lower until the water was lapping around the wood. This was exactly what I wanted as it would help to keep the raft from being washed over the spikes. Or so I hoped.

We were almost on them now. The gap narrowed. I reached out, caught hold of both spikes, and pulled the raft against them. I was half afraid the current would sweep the end of the raft round and over into the Devil's Cup, but it held. For a moment I looked down into the swirling, foaming torrents that raged round and round the bottom of the giant Cup. It was frightening. Terribly frightening. I felt dizzy and looked away. Now and then the raft lurched dangerously, and I knew it could only be a matter of minutes before we were swept over.

'What are we going to do now?' yelled Doubter.

Twisting my head around I nodded towards the wall, and shouted, 'The spikes! Try and lassoo those other spikes — up there on the wall. It's our only chance.'

With trembling hands, Doubter untied the mooring rope, threaded a loop, and started to swing it, cowboy-style, gently around his head. I licked my lips and took a firmer grip.

Curly bit his lower lip nervously. Totey sat up. Tears mingled with the spray that was settling on his face. Round and round Doubter swung the rope. He let go. The loop soared upwards. It dropped on top of the wall but missed and slithered into the Cup. Doubter pulled it back and got ready for another try. This time it settled neatly over a spike. He pulled it tight, and with my help lashed the other end to one of the spikes on the rim of the Cup.

If there are any records for crossing hell-holes like that, I can assure you we broke them. We shinned up the rope quicker than a spider on a thread. Seconds later, the raft lurched for the last time and toppled into the Devil's Cup ... and after it went a lovely big trout, still hooked to our line.

It was only when we turned to jump off the wall that we saw the gamekeeper's son. Dan Moxley was waiting for us. Standing with his hands on his flabby hips, he sneered, 'Well, if it·isn't my old friends!'

'Elephants never forget,' Doubter shot back.

'I never forget poachers or vandals,' replied Dan, 'and this time I've got you. And you haven't got your precious dog to help you get away.'

Desperately I tried to think what we could do. I realised our only hope was to talk Dan into helping us, but we couldn't do that from where we were because of the roar of the water. I started walking along the wall. The others followed, and like a cat stalking mice Dan moved with us. He knew he had us cornered.

About thirty yards along the wall, I judged we were far enough away from the noise and stopped. Dan stepped forward to pull us down, and as he did so I jumped right on top of him. The others needed no urging. They followed suit, and big and all as Dan is, he went down under the sheer weight of numbers. Doubter and Totey grabbed his legs, and Curly and I his arms.

'Now listen, Dan Moxley,' I hissed in his ear as he struggled. 'Now you're going to listen whether you like it or not. We're not poaching, nor are we overturning headstones, no matter what you think.'

'You can tell that to the judge,' he retorted, and tried again to struggle free.

However, we had a good grip of him, and I went on, 'Maybe I have poached here, and then again maybe I haven't, but we didn't come here to poach today. We came to help the Kings.'

'Help the Kings! That's a laugh.'

'Maybe not so much of a laugh as you think,' gritted Curly. 'We came here to warn them that somebody's trying to rob them.'

'Well, it's too late,' panted Dan. 'Somebody's already tried to steal their paintings.' .

'There's more than the paintings at stake,' I told him. 'We believe someone's after the treasure.'

'Don't be daft,' said Dan, turning his head away in disbelief. 'Anyway, they'll never find it.'

'No? Then take a look at this.' I showed him the spade guinea and told him what it was.

Immediately we felt him relax, and he asked, 'Where did you get it?'

'That's what we want to tell Mr. King,' I said. 'Now, if we tell you the whole story, do you promise not to cause any more trouble?'

'I'll do more than that — I'll help you any way I can.'

'Okay,' I said. 'It's a deal.' Whereupon we related the whole chain of events to him.

'And you think if you find whoever's after the treasure, you'll find your friend Cowlick?' he asked when we had finished. We nodded.

'And you think Major Boucher has something to do with it?'

Again we nodded, and he added, 'Come to mention it, he *has* been acting a bit strange lately. So has Miss Felicity for that matter, but then who hasn't with all this business of the ghosts. We've been having ghost trouble at the castle too, you know.'

We told him we had heard about it, and he went on, 'Well, it's getting worse. We can hear all sorts of weird noises at night, and the maids, or what's left of them, have started to sleep out.'

Prince came running up to us and we hugged him, we were so glad to see him.

'What are you going to do now?' asked Dan. 'Do you want to talk to Mr. Rochford-King straightaway?'

'Not yet,' I said. 'We'd like to have a look around first, if it's okay with you, and maybe you could find us something to eat. We're famished.'

We followed Dan through the rhododendron bushes and scrub ash and under the towering ivy-clad trees towards the castle, and we were glad we had won over such a valuable friend.

We didn't really know what we were looking for. The same as before, I suppose — anything odd that might give us a lead. Making sure no one could see us, we made our way across to the boating lake, up the Japanese gardens, and along the fruit gardens and the vegetable gardens to the stables. Dan took great pride in leading the way and letting us know how well he knew his way around the place. I didn't say so, of course, but I knew it every bit as well as he did, and maybe better, on account of my father and myself having hunted there long before Dan ever came. However, I considered this was hardly the time or the place to be making claims of that sort.

We didn't let on to Dan either, but the fruit gardens never looked so tempting. The trees were heavy with apples and pears and it wouldn't be long before they'd be ripe.

The vegetable gardens looked very nice too, and I couldn't help thinking they would have brought a twinkle to Old Daddy Armstrong's eyes if he could have seen them. My own eyes fell on a row of bamboo poles over by the gate. I couldn't make out what they were holding up, but I took a powerful fancy to them, as I could just imagine Cowlick and myself jousting with a couple of them, like real knights in armour. The thought of Cowlick brought me back to earth.

From the gardens Dan took us up along the stables and into the lofts by a back steps. Peering through a wire-mesh window, we could see Felicity supervising a class of pupils who were riding round the stable yard. In a corner of the yard, a workman was giving another horse a fancy haircut with electric clippers. We could see it was Simon Craig, but we knew it couldn't be his blood mare. It was standing too still, and anyway we knew he would never look after his own mare like that. After a few minutes we saw Felicity mount up from an ancient stone mounting block and ride away with her pupils.

There was nothing odd there, so we headed round to the stone tower where, as we had related to Dan, Major Boucher had so mysteriously disappeared.

We were approaching the tower, when who should we see standing in the doorway but the Major himself. What was more, he was talking to the broken-nosed man and his two companions — the very same three who, we believed, had beaten up Juno on Wariff Hill!

After a few minutes they all went into the tower, and we crept closer in the hope of hearing what they were saying. However, when we peered through the long narrow window slits, we were just in time to see them going down through a trapdoor in the floor!

12. SOUNDS IN THE NIGHT

Dan Moxley was as flabbergasted as we were, and when the trapdoor settled into the dust-covered floor of the tower, he exclaimed, 'Pheasants' feathers! Did you see that?'

'Where does it lead to?' Doubter asked him.

'Search me. I never even knew it existed.'

'Well, *we* know these men,' I told him. 'They're the ones we were telling you about. They beat up Gypsy Juno.'

'Do they work here?' asked Doubter.

Dan shook his head. 'I've never seen them before in my life.'

'Then how did they get in without setting off the burglar alarm?' asked Curly.

'That's what I'm wondering,' said Dan.

'It's obvious,' I said. 'Major Boucher must have let them in — probably through one of the green doors in the estate wall. Come on, let's follow and see where they go. And be careful! We don't want to get caught just when we're on to them.'

I held Prince's collar with one hand, and put the other over his nose to keep him quiet, and we stole into the tower. The trapdoor was a lot heavier than we expected, but we could see by the blue smears on the rusted hinges that someone had oiled it recently, and Dan and Doubter were able to raise it without too much difficulty.

A flight of stone steps, worn shallow in the middle by countless footsteps, took us down into a tunnel the height of a man and almost as wide as it was high. It was pitch-dark when we lowered the trapdoor back into place. Luckily I still had my torch. Before switching it on, we listened for any sound of Major Boucher and the three thugs, but there wasn't a sound, except for the steady plop of water dripping somewhere nearby. With my heart thumping, I switched on the torch. The yellow beam cut the musty darkness and sparkled on the glistening dampness of the tunnel stones. Still there was no move, no sound, and cautiously we began edging our way forward.

We could see that the tunnel was very very old. Yet every single stone was still in place, if anything wedged even tighter by the passage of time. As in the steps down to it, a shallow path had been worn in the flag-stones of the tunnel floor.

We realised it must have taken years, maybe centuries, of walking to wear them down like that, and we wondered what it had been used for, and if it dated back to the time of Sir Timothy King. More important, what was it being used for now by Major Boucher and the thugs who had attacked Gypsy Juno, and where did it lead to?

Anxious to find out, we pressed forward. Not knowing what to expect, we kept close together. We were crouched almost double ... partly to guard against hitting our heads against any hidden outcrop, partly to protect ourselves from any other unknown dangers which the darkness of the tunnel might possibly hold for us.

Further along the tunnel, the circle of torchlight lit up

two doorways — one on the left and one on the right. Thinking maybe Major Boucher and the other men had gone into one of them, we switched off the light, crept nearer, paused and listened. There wasn't a sound from either side, so we switched on the light again and went forward. The doors were made of iron bars. They opened inwards and were half open and rusted stiff. Beyond each of them was a small damp stone room with no windows.

'Cells,' I whispered, as the light fell on rusty iron manacles hanging from the back wall. 'And look, there are more up ahead.'

We came upon several more cells, and we couldn't help thinking of the poor souls who had been condemned to rot in them in the dark days of years gone by. So forbidding did we find them, we didn't even venture into them.

At last we came to another flight of stone steps, and we were relieved to see them, for we were beginning to wonder if the tunnel would ever end. I was still holding Prince, so Dan and Doubter crept up the steps first and eased open the trapdoor at the top.

'We're in some kind of room,' whispered Doubter.

Totey sniffed. 'I can smell something cooking.'

'Onions,' said Doubter, who had his nose to the slit of light at the top of the steps.

'You'd better keep quiet,' hissed Curly. 'This might be their hide-out.'

We could see Dan and Doubter easing the trapdoor higher.

'It's not a hide-out,' Dan exclaimed. 'It's the castle kitchen!'

'The castle kitchen?' I said. 'Is there anybody about?'

'Not at the moment,' he told us. 'But wait here until I give the word.'

Quietly he slipped up into the kitchen, and we saw him rummage here, there and everywhere, collecting bread, buns and bottles of milk. Then he tip-toed over to the doors,

peeped out to see if anyone was coming, and waved to us
to come up.

'Now,' he said when we were all crowding closely behind
him, 'follow me, and don't make a sound.'

He led us out, down a long, wide hall, around a corner,
and in through a heavily studded door, to what he later
told us was one of the castle's big square towers. It was
in this end of the castle, he said, that the staff had their
living-quarters.

A few minutes later, in his own small room at the top
of several flights of stone steps, we were hungrily devouring
the food he had brought from the kitchen.

'How come there's nobody about?' I asked him.

'There's never anyone around at this time of day. That's
probably why Major Boucher chose this particular time to
do whatever it is he's doing.'

'I wonder where he took those men?' asked Curly.

'Any one of a thousand places. There are hundreds of
rooms in the castle and a thousand ways to get to them.'

'What are we going to do now?' asked Doubter. 'We'll
never find out anything cooped up in here.'

'Maybe not,' Dan told him, 'but you'll have to stay here
until tonight. The place will be buzzing with activity soon,
and if you go near the kitchen before dinner you'll be spotted
for sure.'

'That suits us fine,' I said before Doubter could say
anything more. 'We couldn't have a better look-out post
than this tower. We can watch at the windows for any
suspicious movement around the castle, and after dark we
can keep an eye on Wariff Hill to see if there are any more
signals.'

'And then?' asked Doubter.

'Then, when everybody else has gone to bed, we'll try
and track down the ghost or whatever's making all the weird
noises Dan's been telling us about. I've a feeling it all has

something to do with the plot to steal the treasure.'

Dan smiled. 'And you have Prince. He just might be able to lead us right to the source of the noise.'

'Exactly,' I said. 'You can't beat a dog when it comes to things like that.'

Doubter, who had been looking out of the window towards the valley, turned towards us, his face creased with worry. 'I don't know. We've been away from home long enough as it is.'

Curly agreed. 'He's right. We *have* been away a long time. We're bound to have been missed by now. Even if we haven't, there'd be blue murder if we didn't go home tonight. And I don't know about you, but my mother and father would be up the walls with worry.'

I nodded. 'Maybe so. But I'm not going home without Cowlick. I'm convinced that whatever or whoever he ran into up on Wariff Hill last night had something to do with the plot to steal the treasure. If I'm right, that means he's being held prisoner. So I don't know about you, but I'm staying here until I get to the bottom of it and find him.'

'Well, when you put it that way, I suppose there's nothing else we can do but stay,' said Doubter. 'What windows will we take?'

Dan left to keep an eye on the kitchen and on Major Boucher, if and when he turned up, and we began our vigil at the small windows of the tower. Mine looked out across the stable yard, and I suppose I was luckier than the others. I was able to watch Felicity putting her pupils through their paces in a small jumping enclosure immediately beyond. How I would have given anything to be astride one of those neatly clipped horses with their fancy bridles and bandaged fetlocks.

As I watched, I began to wonder what connection Felicity could possibly have with this whole mysterious affair. In spite of the business of the bracelet, I couldn't imagine

anyone so beautiful and serene as she is having anything
to do with anything bad. I felt a lot better after I had settled
that in my mind, and I went on to think about her father.
What would she do when she learned that her father, the
most trusted man on the whole castle staff, was mixed up
in — maybe even the brains behind — a plot to rob the
man she loved and planned one day to marry? I only hoped
that when she found out, she wouldn't go and drown herself
in the Devil's Cup like that other poor broken-hearted girl
Old Daddy Armstrong had told us about.

After a while it began to rain, and Felicity led her pupils
back to the stables. There I saw them rub down the horses
and give them everything short of a hot bath before even
going indoors to get dried out themselves, and I just thought
again that anyone who could be so good to animals as Felicity
was, couldn't do anything bad.

The view from my window seemed very bleak after they
had gone in. The boating lake was dimpled and dull from
the steady patter of rain, and the magnificent white statues
that adorn the lawns looked wet and miserable. Even my
favourite one, Diana the goddess of hunting, seemed dark
and disheartened. It was my father who told me about her
one day when we were doing a bit of hunting in the estate
ourselves. You wouldn't think he would know things like
that, being only a road-worker, but then that's him.

None of us saw anything suspicious, although we hardly
took our eyes away from the windows once. It was beginning
to get dark when Dan came back. He had more food for
us, but no news worth talking about. Major Boucher hadn't
come around the kitchen all afternoon, and the kitchen
gossip, while all about ghosts, yielded nothing that would
help us in any way.

When we had eaten, we settled down to watch Wariff
Hill, each of us taking turns at the window that looks out
towards it. After I had done my spell, I lay down on Dan's

bed and closed my eyes and listened to the rain. Before
I knew it, I was thinking about what Doubter and Curly
had said about the worry we would be causing at home.
Normally our house is very warm and peaceful. When my
father has everything closed in for the night, he puts on
his slippers and sits in the armchair with his feet crossed
in front of the fire, the back of his head almost touching
the big shiny brass weights of the wag-at-the-wall clock on
the wall behind him. Some nights Mr. Stockman calls over
and my mother makes them a cup of tea.

It wouldn't be like that tonight, I thought. Our fathers
would all be in, and a lot of other neighbours, and they'd
be talking and wondering where we had gone. My mother
would be sitting on the sofa sniffing into her handkerchief,
worrying herself sick. My father knew I could look after
myself and would tell her so.

Still, it was in her nature to worry. I often heard my
father telling her she wouldn't be happy unless she had
something to worry about. However, that was when she
was worrying over small things that weren't worth worrying
over. I didn't like giving her the anxiety she was bound
to be feeling now, but what else could I do? Anyway, she
wouldn't be as concerned as if I was missing on my own.
That went for all our folks. They'd know we were off on
some escapade together. They'd be trying to figure out where
we could be and where to start searching. Knowing my
father, I felt sure he'd get them to start with the plantation
and cover the valley methodically, just the way he covers
a field when he's trying to rise a rabbit.

I must have dozed off, for the next thing I knew the
boys were shaking me. 'What is it?' I whispered. 'Did you
see the light again?'

'Not a move on Wariff Hill tonight,' said Doubter. 'But
listen ...'

'Can't you hear it?' asked Dan, his ear cocked at the door.

I strained my ears. For a moment I could hear nothing except our own breathing. Then I heard it. A distant jangle of chains. 'What is it?' I asked him.

'That's it.'

'You mean the weird noise you've been hearing?'

Dan nodded. 'What do you make of it?'

I listened to the noise again. 'It's like ... like the noise a prisoner would make in one of the cells we saw ... pacing up and down, dragging his chains after him.'

'It fits all right,' Curly agreed.

'What do the staff think it is?' I asked Dan.

'Some of them think it's the running dead man of the legend ...'

'And what do the others think?' asked Curly.

'They think it's the tormented soul of Sir Timothy ... that it can never rest because of what he did to his daughter.'

'That sounds a bit far-fetched,' said Doubter.

'You wouldn't think that if you had to lie here night after night listening to it,' replied Dan. 'And the maids are not the only ones who are convinced it's one or the other. I heard Major Boucher himself debating it with the butler the other day.'

'Would there be anybody around now?' I asked him.

'Not on your life.'

'What about Mr. King?' asked Doubter.

'Mr. Rochford-King,' said Dan, pointedly giving him his correct name, 'did a lot of looking for it at first, but he got nowhere, and now he just says he has more important things to do then waste time looking for ghosts.'

'Come on then,' I said. 'Let's see what *we* can find.'

I held on to Prince to keep him from running ahead of us, and we followed Dan out and down the stone steps. We could hear the chains a lot louder now. Hugging close to Dan, we found ourselves creeping along corridor after corridor, trying to get closer to that continual, restless jangle.

Each time we got to where we thought it had been, however, it seemed to be where we had just left.

'This is like chasing the will-o'-the-wisp in the Cottonbog,' I whispered to Dan.

'I know,' came the reply from the darkness immediately in front of me. 'What do you want to do?'

'Let's stay here for a minute and listen.'

We were now in a gloomy corridor, from the dark recesses of which stags' heads stared down at us with unseeing eyes.

'Where are we anyway?' asked Doubter.

'We're in the Stags' Hall.'

'The what?' asked Totey.

'The Stags' Hall,' whispered Dan. 'Can't you see the antlers on the walls?'

'Shush,' I said, and standing perfectly still, we listened intently. Not another sound disturbed the darkness but that floating, ghostly jangle. Then we heard footsteps too. Our hearts were thumping, and we were almost stepping on each other's heels and toes as we edged closer together. Totey held on tightly to my jacket, and I held on tightly to Prince. One minute the chains would jangle away off somewhere, next minute they sounded close at hand. The footsteps came and went with the chains, a dull sort of plodding that stopped now and then, and always started up again with each fresh jangle of chains.

'Does this go on all night?' I asked Dan.

'Only for the first hour after midnight.'

'Every night?' asked Doubter.

Before Dan could answer, there was one almighty jangle close beside us. Startled, we shrank back. As we did so, Prince snarled and barked, and if we were surprised by that last jangle, it was nothing to our surprise at what happened next.

When Prince barked, we heard a stumble and another jangle, almost as if someone else had got a fright and jumped

back too, and, lo and behold, if we didn't hear the sound
of running footsteps accompanied by the continuous jangle
of a trailing chain.

After that, there wasn't a single sound to be heard in
the whole castle, and hardly able to contain our excitement
we hurried back up to Dan's room.

'Well that's the first time I ever heard of a ghost being
frightened by a dog,' I said when we had closed the door
and put on the light.

Curly flopped into one of the chairs. 'What do you make
of it so?'

'I don't think it's any more a ghost than what we saw
up on Wariff Hill.'

'Neither do I,' said Doubter.

I sat down on the edge of the bed, for I was still feeling
weak at the knees. 'I think it's all part and parcel of the
plan to steal the treasure.'

'How do you make that out?' asked Dan.

'Well, look at it this way. It must have been a man we
heard running away. If that's so, it can only mean one thing.
Somebody's going to an awful lot of trouble to make people
think the castle is haunted.'

'But why?' wondered Totey.

'Maybe to cover up for something,' I suggested.

'Like digging for the treasure,' said Curly.

'Exactly. It would cover up any noise they made — and
come to think of it, it would make the staff stay clear of
this part of the castle, at least for an hour each night.'

'So the question is,' said Doubter, 'what's on the other
side of that wall?'

'That's the problem,' said Dan. 'There's nothing on the
other side of it. That's the outside wall of the castle.'

13. KIDNAPPED

We were dumbfounded. We *had* heard a man running. We were sure of it. For a moment an awful thought occurred to me. Could it really have been the ghost of Sir Timothy or the running dead man of the legend after all? I tried to put such thoughts aside. No, it couldn't be.

'What about the rooms around the Stags' Hall?' I asked Dan. 'What's above it?'

'Let me see — yes — the Bouchers live on that floor.'

'The Bouchers!' I exclaimed. 'Then maybe we're not so far wrong after all.'

'But what can we do?' asked Doubter.

'I don't know,' I said. 'Unless we could steal a look at Major Boucher's rooms. What do you think, Dan?'

'Well ... I suppose we could. He's always busy in the mornings.'

It was at least another hour before we settled down for the night. We had discussed how we would go about getting into Major Boucher's rooms, the ghost, the treasure, the

Legend of the Golden Key, and, of course, poor Cowlick.
Our anxiety for him was mounting and we wished for the
morning to come so that we could push on and get to the
bottom of this whole mysterious affair.

Totey slept in the single bed with Dan, Doubter and
Curly snuggled into a couple of old armchairs, and Prince
and I curled up on a rug near the bed. In normal
circumstances, I suppose we would have put in a restless
night, but it had been a long day and we were tired, and
in spite of the discomfort we slept soundly.

Next morning, Dan brought us up more food from the
kitchen after he had his own breakfast, and as we tucked
into it, he went out again to check on Major Boucher's
whereabouts. When he came back he told us that the Major
was still downstairs, and now would be as good a time as
any to have a look at his rooms. Half way down the stone
steps, he took us through a little doorway in the side of
the tower, and we found ourselves in a wing of bedrooms.
He led us along a corridor, round a corner, up a short flight
of stairs and then along another corridor, until at last we
came to a set of rooms facing on to a wide curving staircase.
We took a quick look over the green marble banister into
the hall below. There was no one about. Dan stepped back
quickly and tried the handle of the nearest door. It opened,
and we all hurried inside.

'Okay, let's try the walls for secret doors,' I whispered,
and pointing to a connecting door added, 'We'll do that
room first, and then this one.'

Without further delay, we descended upon the adjoining
room, which we discovered was a bedroom. Round the walls
we went, sounding them with our knuckles, and twisting
any knobs we could find in or about the big open fire-
lace. We came up with nothing there to suggest Major
Boucher had some secret means of haunting the castle, and
we quickly moved back out to the other room.

While the others continued to sound the walls, I took a look at Major Boucher's writing-desk. It was one of those antique ones, with a front that rolls open and shut, and dozen of small drawers inside. Starting at the top, I worked my way down through the drawers on the left, then on the right. Imagine my surprise when, in the bottom right-hand drawer, I found Felicity's missing bracelet! It was underneath a sheaf of tattered yellow papers. Furthermore, the faded writing on the papers was about the Legend of the Golden Key and the treasure. There were also what looked like rough, hand-drawn maps with X's here and circles there, and straight and squiggly lines in between.

I called the others, but no sooner had they peeped at what I had found than the door opened, and we turned around to come face to face with Major Boucher!

Angrily he demanded to know what we were doing in his room. We could see Dan trying desperately to think of an excuse, and after some hesitation he told the Major that we were his friends and that he was just showing us around the castle. The Major looked at his writing-desk and then at us again. I could see he didn't know what to make of us. Finally, he told us curtly we had no business being in his rooms, and ordered us out.

I knew Prince didn't like anyone talking to us like that, so I lifted him up in my arms to keep him under control. As Major Boucher ushered us down the stairs, I couldn't help wondering if he had seen us at the drawer, or if I had closed it in time. Whether he had or not, it was obvious from the way he was rushing us that he was anxious to see us out of the castle.

At the entrance to the Stags' Hall, however, we ran straight into Mr. King. He was wearing riding clothes, and we guessed he was on his way out to the stables.

'I say, who are these chaps?' he asked in the grandest accent you ever heard.

'Friends of young Moxley here,' growled Major Boucher. 'I'm just showing them out.'

Now was the time, I though. It had to be now or never, and as Mr. King was about to walk on, I blurted out, 'Excuse me!'

He turned. 'Yes, boy?'

'The treasure,' I said. 'We came to warn you!'

'Oh come, come,' said Major Boucher, pulling me away. 'We haven't time to be listening to your fairy tales.'

'Just a minute, Major,' said Mr. King, coming back to me. 'What's that you say about the treasure?'

'Someone's trying to steal it,' I told him. 'That's why we came here — to warn you.'

'Such nonsense,' snapped Major Boucher. 'Come now, out with you all.'

'It's not nonsense,' I cried. 'It's true, and I have something that can prove it.'

Major Boucher was fuming, but Mr. King, I could see, wasn't going to be put off now. 'Very well,' he said, 'follow me. We can talk about this in my study and see whatever you say you have, young man. There's better light in there . . .and, good grief boy, *do* put down that dog.'

I suppose I did look a bit silly carrying Prince, but when I put him down he dashed off in the direction of the kitchen. I made to go after him, then thought I'd better stick with the others who were following Major Boucher and Mr. King out of the hall. In that split second of hesitation, I felt a draught at the back of my neck, and before I could turn around, a hand clamped over my mouth and I was hauled back into complete darkness.

Someone tied my hands behind my back, and I was carried along a passage so narrow my elbows brushed against both walls. I could feel myself being taken down flight after flight of steps. At the bottom I was put on my feet. I heard the bolt of a door being drawn back, and I was thrown into some sort of room, where I stumbled and fell on a heap of straw.

As the door clanged shut behind me and my eyes began to adjust to the darkness, I became aware of a figure kneeling beside me.

'Tapser,' exclaimed a familiar voice.

'Cowlick,' I cried. 'Cowlick, is that you?'

To my utter delight, I found it was none other.

No one could imagine how glad I was to see Cowlick alive and well. If my hands hadn't been tied behind my back, I would have thrown my arms around him and hugged him, and I'm sure he'd have done the same if his hands had been free.

'What on earth happened to you?' I asked as I struggled to sit up.

'Obviously the same thing that's happened to you — I was caught by those crooks who are after the treasure.' Cowlick shook his head and blew upwards to dislodge a piece of straw caught in his cow's-lick curl. 'You remember when we spread out around Wariff Hill? Well, I was pushing my way through the briars when I tripped and fell headlong. My head must have hit a stone. The next thing I knew, I woke up in some sort of cave. It was dark, except for a candle on a box beside me. I was bound and gagged, and the broken-nosed man and his two friends were standing over me.'

'I just thought it was them,' I said. 'We saw them here yesterday with Major Boucher. Was it them who threw me in here? I couldn't see in the dark?'

'It was, but there are more in this business besides them and Major Boucher. Anyway, as I was saying, when I woke up the three of them were standing over me. I heard some of you calling me with your bourtree whistle, and I started to struggle and shout as loud as I could through the gag, but one of them held me still and made me be quiet. I could see them listening to see if they had been heard, so the cave must have been pretty near the fort. After a while one of them went out, and when he came back he said the rest of you had gone. They warned me not to shout or it would be the worse for me, and then they took the gag off and started to question me.'

'What did they want to know?' I asked.

'What we were doing there.'

'What did you tell them?'

'I told them we were lamping rabbits. I just thought of that on the spur of the moment, and I suppose it sounded reasonable enough. Anyway, they seemed to believe it. The one with the broken nose told one of the others to search me, and when he found nothing the broken-nosed man asked me if we had found anything on the hill.'

'The spade guinea!' I exclaimed.

'Exactly ... but I pretended I didn't know what he was talking about. I could see they didn't want to give anything away, so I kept up the innocent act, and in the end they seemed satisfied that I really didn't know what they were talking about.'

'I wonder what they would have done if they had found you with the guinea, Cowlick?'

'I don't know, but it didn't make much difference. They wouldn't let me go. I told them that if they let me go I wouldn't say a word about it to a soul, as I wasn't supposed to be out that late anyway. They just told me to shut my trap. So I told them that if they didn't let me go, they'd soon be caught as everybody in the valley would be out looking for me. They only laughed and said I wasn't going anywhere until they said so, and not to kid myself, that anybody searching for me would have about as much hope of catching them as they would of catching the running dead man.'

'What happened after that?'

'They blindfolded me. There was a pile of picks and shovels in the cave, and I could hear them lifting them and taking them with them.'

'Why blindfold you?' I wondered.

'They obviously didn't want me to see what they were up to, but from the sounds they made I could tell they didn't leave the cave by the small entrance one of them used when he had a look around outside. While they were away, I tried to free myself but couldn't. It must have been hours before they came back. Something must have happened, because I heard one of them saying it had ruined everything and they would have to tell the boss. So off they set, taking me with them.'

Cowlick paused for a moment before continuing, 'It was still raining when we left Wariff Hill, and I was slipping and sliding all over the place with the blindfold on me. Finally, I suppose when they thought I would have lost my bearings, they took it off. They weren't far wrong either. It was a bit better without the blindfold. At least I could sort of gauge when I was going to go uphill and when I was going to go down. But I couldn't make out where on earth I was, until I heard the sound of falling water and came to a building. I knew then they were taking me into the stone tower here on the estate. There's a trapdoor in the floor of it, and a secret tunnel . . .'

'I know,' I said. 'We followed Major Boucher and the three of them into it yesterday.'

'Well, you know the cells along it? They brought me into one of them, and through a hole in the back of it into the passageway here. Then they locked me in this cell. I've been here ever since.'

'You must be famished,' I said.

'I would have been, if it hadn't been for Major Boucher. He has brought me something to eat two or three times.'

'Poor Felicity,' I said. 'What will she do when she discovers her father is the head of a gang that's stolen the treasure?'

'Who's going to tell her? Unless we escape from here. And another thing ... they haven't found the treasure. They're still digging for it down the passageway. Furthermore, I don't think Major Boucher *is* the head of the gang.'

'You don't?'

'No,' said Cowlick. 'When he brought me food the last time, he was on his own, and he whispered to me not to worry. He said he'd see that no harm would come to me, and not to be frightened by the strange noises I'd be hearing during the night.'

'Then who do you think *is* the boss?'

Cowlick shrugged. 'Marcus ... Wilson Harper ... or any one of the ex-convicts on the estate. Maybe they're all in on it, for all we know.'

'Even so,' I said, 'Felicity still won't be able to marry Mr. King.'

'You can say that again. But I still can't understand why her father should help me when he's helping them, and there's no doubt about it, he's helping them every way he can.'

'Maybe,' I said, 'he doesn't mind stealing, but draws the line at kidnapping or murder. After all, he must know the others are hardened criminals and that they would stop at nothing short of murder to get the gold. Look what they did to poor Juno.'

'That's probably it all right,' said Cowlick, 'but it's still a pretty low thing to do — I mean, robbing your own daughter.'

I had to agree. 'That's what it amounts to all right. When she became Mrs. Rochford-King the treasure would belong to her too.'

Cowlick shifted to a more comfortable position. 'But you

haven't told me what happened to you? Where are the others, and Prince?'

'Don't worry, they're all right,' I assured him. 'They're up in the castle at this very moment — telling Mr. King everything that happened, I hope.'

I told Cowlick the whole story, from the time he disappeared on Wariff Hill, to the moment I was seized in the Stags' Hall and thrown in beside him.

'But you all might have been drowned in the Devil's Cup,' he said when I had finished.

I nodded. 'But how else could we get into the estate without setting off the burglar alarm?'

'I wonder why it didn't go off when broken-nose and his pals brought me in?'

'Major Boucher probably had it switched off, or else he left one of the green doors in the estate wall open for them.'

'That would be it all right,' said Cowlick. 'I thought I heard them shutting a gate or something behind us. It was after that I fell and nearly broke my neck. We must have been going over that bit of ground near the boundary wall, with all the humps and hollows and the steep paths in among the rhododendrons.'

'Little wonder they had to take your blindfold off.'

'Shh,' warned Cowlick, 'somebody's coming.'

'And I've still got the spade guinea in my pocket,' I gasped.

14.   A SIGHT TO BEHOLD

The door was unlocked and the three men came into the cell. One of them, who was carrying an old hurricane lamp, was saying to the broken-nosed man, 'I tell you, we had to take him. He was going to spill the beans to Rochford-King, and he said he had something to prove it.'

'On your feet, both of you,' ordered the broken-nosed man. 'All right, Ginger, where are you from?'

'From the valley,' I said. 'And my name's not Ginger.'

'Don't be smart,' he snarled. 'What were you doing up in the castle?'

'Playing with Dan Moxley.'

'Snooping, you mean. What were you going to show Rochford-King.'

'Nothing.'

'No? Search him!'

One of the others stepped forward and started to go through my pockets. In my jacket pocket he came across my bourtree whistle and my torch. He gave the torch to the broken-nosed man and threw the whistle aside with hardly a glance. In my trousers pocket, of course, he found the guinea.

'So,' said the broken-nosed man, shining my torch on it, 'you were only playing, huh?' Giving the torch to one of the others, he struck me across the face with the back of his hand.

'Leave him alone,' shouted Cowlick as I staggered under the blow. 'Leave him alone, or it'll be the worse for you.'

The broken-nosed man ignored him and came after me. 'How much do you know?' he demanded, hitting me again.

My face was stinging, and I could taste blood on my lips as I reeled against the wall of the cell.

'How much do you know?' he repeated, catching my jacket and holding me up against the wall.

'What is there to know about an oul' halfpenny I found up on Wariff Hill,' I yelled back at him.

'Trying to be smart, eh?' he snarled, raising his hand to hit me again.

I cringed, but before the blow could fall another figure came into the cell. It was Major Boucher.

'Stop it, stop it at once,' he demanded, throwing himself in front of me.

'Stand aside, old man, or you'll get it too,' threatened the broken-nosed man.

'No,' said Major Boucher in a trembling, but determined voice. 'You're to get on with the job as quickly as possible — that's an order. What does it matter what they know? By the time they're found you'll be far away — if you've the sense to get on with it.'

For a moment they stared at each other. Then the broken-nosed man relaxed, pocketed the guinea and strode out, followed by the other two. I slid to the floor, weak and trembling, and found Major Boucher untying my hands. He also untied Cowlick's hands, and giving him his handkerchief told him, 'Here, dab his face with this. I'll be back in a moment.'

When the Major returned, he hung a hurricane lamp on the wall outside and brought in a bowl of hot water with which he cleaned and bathed the cuts and bruises on my face.

'Don't worry, old chap,' he said. 'I have my own plans for those ruffians.'

Before we could ask him any questions, we heard someone coming.

'Pretend you're still tied,' he whispered, and we whipped our hands behind us again.

'Okay, Major,' said the man with the broken nose. 'We need your help — come on!'

'All right, all right,' said Major Boucher.

When they went out the broken-nosed man locked the door and they disappeared down the passageway.

'How do you feel now?' asked Cowlick.

'A lot better than I would have if Major Boucher hadn't intervened. I wonder if they're still within earshot?'

'There's one way to find out,' said Cowlick, and he proceded to shout, 'Help! Help!'

There wasn't a sound from the passageway.

'Now's our chance,' I said. 'Have you got your bourtree whistle?'

Cowlick shook his head. 'I squashed it when I fell up at the fairy fort.'

'Then help me find mine.'

Scrambling on to our hands and knees, we started picking through the straw. In spite of the light from the passageway, it was still quite gloomy in the cell and we couldn't remember just where my whistle had been thrown.

'If we could signal with it,' I continued, 'they just might hear us up in the castle, and Prince and the boys would know immediately it was one of us looking for help.'

'Good idea,' said Cowlick, 'but where did it fall?'

'I've got it, I've got it,' I cried. 'Here, you blow it, my lips are too sore.'

Pressing his face in between the bars of the cell door, Cowlick blew three sharp blasts on the whistle. We listened. There was no reply. Again he put the whistle to his lips ... and again ... and again ... 'It's no good,' he said at last. 'They can't hear us.'

'Listen,' I said. 'I thought I heard Prince. Try once more.'

Again Cowlick put the whistle to his lips and blew three times. Hardly had the echo died away than we heard three faint answering blasts away above us in the castle.

'They've heard us, they've heard us,' I cried. 'Keep it up, keep it up.'

Soon the whistling was joined by loud hammering, and

we guessed Mr. King and the boys had been guided to the Stags' Hall by our signals and were looking for the secret door. Even as we were rejoicing, we heard the men returning. Quickly we threw ourselves down on the straw and put our hands behind our backs. As we did so, the three of them appeared at the door. They looked in, then looked up, and listened.

'It's coming from the Stags' Hall,' said one.

The broken-nosed man nodded and said, 'Quick, we must look for the boss. Whoever finds him first, tell him they're on to us and that we'll have to make the breakthrough now.'

They hurried off, and when the sound of their footsteps had died away Cowlick continued to blow the whistle to guide Mr. King and the boys and, we hoped, spur them on to greater efforts. All the while, the barking and the whistling and the hammering continued above us. We hoped against hope that they would find the secret door and break through before the thieves returned, but not so.

After only a few minutes, we heard the men running back into the passageway and start hammering at something with implements, probably picks and sledgehammers, we thought.

Next thing we knew, someone else entered the passageway and an argument developed. We pressed our faces between the bars and squinted to our utmost, but we couldn't see what was happening. Seconds later, we saw Major Boucher being propelled along the passageway by the broken-nosed man. The Major was resisting for all he was worth, and when he was almost opposite our cell he managed to break free and make a run for the steps leading up to where we reckoned the secret door must be in the Stags' Hall.

Our hearts were in our mouths as we watched him scramble up the steep steps on all fours. We hoped desperately that he would make it, but the broken-nosed man, who was younger and stronger, caught him and pulled him back. Another struggle ensued at the bottom of the steps, and to our horror, we saw Major Boucher go down under a hail of blows.

Without even checking to see if he was alive or dead, the broken-nosed man then turned and dashed back to where his friends were still digging for the gold.

'Major Boucher, Major Boucher,' we cried.

He didn't stir.

'Major Boucher, Major Boucher.'

To our great relief, we saw him lift his head and look in our direction.

'Major Boucher,' I called again. 'Are you all right?'

He didn't answer, but pushed himself up on to his hands and knees and began creeping over to us. Away above us the banging had got louder and we guessed they had found the secret door and were trying to break it in. At the same time, the hammering down the passageway had speeded up to a frenzied clatter. Major Boucher was outside the cell door now. We reached through the bars and helped him to his feet. He staggered along the wall, and when he reappeared he had the key to the cell door.

With trembling hands we helped him to unlock it.

As we tumbled out into the passageway, Mr. King and some of his men came bounding down the steps, followed by Dan, Doubter, Curly and Totey. We cried out a greeting to them, and threw an anxious glance down the passageway to where the crooks were working.

The sight that met our eyes rooted us to the spot, for we had turned just in time to see none other than Simon Craig lay open a secret niche in the passage wall with one final swing of a pick. As he did so, an ancient iron-banded casket crashed on to a pile of rubble and burst open. However, it didn't spill out the stream of glittering gold coins that we expected. Instead out fell one single solitary spade guinea, which rolled slowly around in a circle before collapsing and shivering to a stop on the dusty floor.

15.   DUEL ON THE HILL

'I don't believe it,' exclaimed Doubter from the steps. Like Mr. King and the others, he had stopped, mesmerised by what he had seen.

Craig immediately dropped the pick and tried to grab the casket. However, his three helpers apparently had the same idea. A mad scramble ensued. Two of them were sent flying on the floor, to be seized by the powerful arms of Marcus who had come down the steps with Mr. King.

Realising there was nothing for it now but to escape without the treasure, Craig and the broken-nosed man fled through a large hole that had been made in the side of the tunnel. Mr. King grabbed a hurricane lamp they had been using, and following him through the hole we found ourselves in the other tunnel leading from the kitchen to the stone tower.

Prince was by my side now and as we hurried along the tunnel I reached down and patted his neck. A few minutes later we climbed up into the tower and rushed outside. As we did so, we saw Craig disappearing round the corner of the stables, and the broken-nosed man racing away through the trees.

'Go seek'm, boy,' I yelled, and Prince needed no second bidding. As he streaked off in pursuit of the broken-nosed man, we followed Mr. King towards the stables. At the entrance to the stable yard, we had to take a quick step back when Craig came charging out on his blood mare. He swerved, almost ran down the foreman, Wilson Harper, who tried to stop him, and cut through the vegetable gardens. There he slowed down for a moment to grab one of the long bamboo poles, before galloping on through the far gate, where he swerved savagely back into the trees and made off in the direction of Big Hughie's farm.

As Mr. King had been on his way out to the stables when we met him, his horse was already saddled and waiting for him. Seeing Craig gallop off he sprang into the saddle, also collected one of the bamboo poles on the way through the vegetable gardens, and raced off through the trees in pursuit. At that moment, to add to the confusion, the burglar alarm began clanging throughout the castle, triggered, no doubt, by the broken-nosed man clambering over the boundary wall.

'Come on,' cried Dan. 'Up to my room. We can watch from there.'

Panting for breath, we flung ourselves over to the window of Dan's room. And what a sight met our eyes! Big Hughie's farm was like a battle-field. The broken-nosed man had run into a long line of men coming down the back field towards the estate and we knew it was a search-party out looking for us. I picked out my father, Mr. Stockman and Juno. Even Shouting Sam was there, his gramophone horn raised to his lips as if urging his troops into battle.

The broken-nosed man turned, only to be confronted by Prince, who obviously had been delayed trying to get over the wall. He started kicking, but that only made Prince leap upon him and seize his trouser leg. The searchers moved in on him, and that's when he made his second mistake. He threw a punch at my father. The broken-nosed man was big, but so is my father. He just drew back, and if he didn't break that ruffian's nose again he must have broken his jaw, for he sent him reeling down the field.

'Oh, boy, did you see that?' I exclaimed, throwing up my fists at Cowlick. 'Wham, just like that!'

'There's Craig now,' shouted Dan, and we crowded around the window again in time to see the searchers waving their arms to try and stop the blood mare. The mare reared up, but Craig held on and turned her back towards the estate.

Through a gap in the trees, we could see Mr. King take his mount clear over the estate wall at a spot where Craig's mare had dislodged some stones. Gathering up his horse in fine style, he raced up the field to cut Craig off. Then we saw the strangest spectacle of all.

Levelling their bamboo poles like lances, the two horsemen charged each other like knights of old. Never before had we seen anything like it, except in books or on television, and we watched wide-eyed as they warded each other off to survive the first clash.

Turning sharply, they faced each other again. This time Craig caught Mr. King a glancing blow on the shoulder. Being an expert rider, Mr. King held on, for all the world like a whitterick clinging to the neck of a rabbit. Then without even pausing to rub his shoulder, he swung around to face Craig for a third time.

Both spurred their horses forward. They met. Mr. King caught Craig squarely on the shoulder with his bamboo, and to our great delight we saw Craig swept clean off his blood mare, to be promptly seized by members of the search party. As I said before, we weren't the only ones who needed riding-lessons.

It wasn't long before Craig and his three friends were safely locked up in one of the castle cells awaiting the arrival of the police. Mr. King invited everyone else into the castle, and with the large crowd gathered around a huge mahogany table we related our story.

Our fathers were very pleased with us when they heard it — so much so that my father offered me a cigarette. I didn't take it, of course, just in case he was trying me out for I know he doesn't approve of young people smoking. Still, I knew he was very proud of me, and I was just as proud of him for the way he despatched the man with the broken nose.

For their part, they had guessed we might be at the castle after Gypsy Juno told them about our visit to his mother and Mr. Stockman told them about the raft.

Major Boucher filled us in on the rest of the story. Why, you might ask, was he with us and not in the cells with the other four crooks, and what happened to the treasure? As the Major himself explained, he *was* after the treasure all right, but not for the same reason as the others. He sat back, relaxed, the centre of all attention.

'You see,' he said, 'I know how much Felicity and Mr. Rochford-King want to get married, and I knew they wouldn't be able to afford it for a long time to come, what with costs rising all round, and the income of the estate barely sufficient to meet them. So I decided to make a serious effort to solve the Legend of the Golden Key in an endeavour to secure for them the long-lost treasure. I searched through all the books in the castle library, and studied every possible reference to either the treasure or the legend. I studied and studied them until I could barely sleep at night for thinking about the legend. I even studied the exact wording of it as inscribed on Sir Timothy's headstone, and examined every grave in the family cemetery.'

We didn't interrupt, but we realised then that the figure

Shouting Sam had seen 'rising' out of Sir Timothy's grave had been the Major. We smiled to ourselves as it dawned on us why Sam had said the figure was 'sort of' dressed like himself. The similarity, of course, was between the Major's plus-fours and Sam's trousers which are wrapped in strips of sacking from the knees down.

'I tried everything,' said Major Boucher, 'but I got nowhere, absolutely nowhere — until Craig came to my room one night.'

'And we thought all the time it was Marcus,' said Cowlick.

'Poor Marcus,' smiled Mr. King. 'His only crime is that he doesn't know his own strength. That's what landed him in prison in the first instance. Cracked some fellow's skull. Probably deserved it.'

Major Boucher continued. 'How Craig tumbled to it I don't know, but he showed me a spade guinea which he had found across there in Mr. McIlhagga's field one day while ploughing. Then the rogue produced Felicity's bracelet which he had stolen to prove that the coins were the same. I saw red, of course, and told him I'd report the matter to Mr. Rochford-King at once, but he was ready with his answer. He said that if I did, he would maintain that it was I who was trying to steal the treasure, not him.'

Major Boucher sighed. 'I knew Mr. Rochford-King would never believe that, but knowing Felicity I was afraid she would refuse to marry him with any hint of suspicion hanging over my head.'

'Oh, father,' said Felicity, 'and I thought *I* was worried about *you*.' She was sitting against the arm of his chair, and she squeezed his shoulder affectionately.

'So,' continued Major Boucher, 'I agreed to help Craig, but with the idea that I'd use him to find the treasure and then turn him over to the police at the last moment. However, as you know, he would have got the better of me had it not been for these lads here.'

'But how on earth did you find the secret tunnel?' asked Mr. King.

'Well,' said Major Boucher, 'it was through Craig really. I don't know how the guinea he found came to be over there in Mr. McIlhagga's field. Perhaps Sir Timothy dropped it while inspecting the ground above the tunnel. Who knows? But you know how these things sometimes turn up, especially when a field is being ploughed.

'In any case, there was no doubt about it, it was a spade guinea, and, what was more, it was of the very same year as the one on Felicity's bracelet. So I decided to work on the assumption that its location was of some significance. The only thing I could see about it, however, was that if I drew a line from the castle through the approximate spot where Craig said he found it, the line cut across the nearest landmark — the mound, or fairy fort as it's called, on Wariff Hill.

'Then, on checking with the museum in Belfast, I was told that Wariff Hill used to have an old Gaelic name.'

He showed us a piece of paper with the words, *Tuama an Fhir Mhairbh,* written on it.

'The pronunciation of it,' he went on, 'is Thooama un irr Wariv, and that no doubt is how Wariff Hill got its name.'

'But what does it mean?' I asked him.

'Ah, that's the point. It means the Mound of the Dead Man. It's a burial mound — not a fort.'

'Bedad you're right,' said Juno, who, as I said before, speaks a bit of Irish. '*Tuama*'s the Irish for tomb or mound,'

'Ah, yes,' said Mr. King, 'probably from the Latin *tumulus*, meaning the same thing.'

Major Boucher nodded and continued, 'Like everyone else, I never had any reason before to consider the mound of the fairy fort as anything but what its name implied — a fort. And, of course, I had no way of knowing what it was called in Sir Timothy's time.

'Nevertheless,' he said, flicking back his drooping white moustache with his forefinger, and obviously feeling rather proud of himself, 'I knew I had at last discovered the 'dead man' of the Legend of the Golden Key. I also discovered that burial mounds in this country have entrance passages to quite large chambers. There are many mounds, or passage graves as they are sometimes called, the best examples being at Newgrange in County Meath. Many of the country's smaller mounds, of course, haven't been excavated yet, but I realised that if the mound on Wariff Hill had been opened in Sir Timothy's time, the entrance shouldn't be too difficult to find.

'Those three thugs Craig hired went to the hill, and sure enough they succeeded in unearthing an entrance to the mound beneath a clump of briars and rubble.'

'So that was the cave I was in?' said Cowlick.

The Major nodded.

'And the lights we saw were theirs?' said Doubter.

'Yes, most probably. They used the old farm-house in the meadow as their headquarters, and it was they who beat up poor Juno here in the belief that he had found Craig's guinea which they had so carelessly dropped.

'Anyway, as I was saying, they found the entrance. What was more, they found that a deep shaft had been sunk in the earthen floor of the chamber. Climbing down an old iron ladder attached to the side of it, they discovered a tunnel going off in the direction of the castle. However, the tunnel had caved in not far from the castle. So, while they worked to clear it, I began a search here to see if I could find the entrance at this end.

'I began to tap the back wall systematically. That's when Mr. King came across me one night in the library, and I'm afraid I made up that story about the attempt to steal the paintings. After that, I couldn't risk being caught at the wall again, especially in the middle of the night, so I tried it from another angle.

'I had discovered the tunnel running from the stone tower to the kitchen. It had been used, I think, in olden days as the way by which staff could come and go without being seen. Somehow I felt it might just run near the other tunnel, and I was right. When we broke through the back of one of the cells, there it was. It was easy to find the secret door from the inside. As you've seen, there are stone steps leading right up to it in the middle of the wall of the Stags' Hall.'

'But how did you know where the treasure-chest was?' asked Cowlick.

'Well,' he explained, 'there was no sign of it anywhere else in the tunnel, and according to tradition it had been hidden outside the castle but *within the estate,* so we realised it had to be in the section that had caved in. You know the rest of the story. The digging was done under cover of the ghost affair. Craig had initiated that earlier as a cover for any noise that might be made in the search for the treasure, and to keep the castle as deserted as possible at night.'

'And what about the bracelet?' I asked.

'Very simple, really,' said Major Boucher. 'I told Felicity she had most probably lost it in the fall up in the plantation, not realising, of course, that she was wearing it in the newspaper photograph taken afterwards on the night of the gymkhana, which you spotted, Tapser.

'At the same time, as you lads also discovered, I did succeed in recovering it, and was trying to think of a suitable place to put it where she would find it without suspecting anything.'

'If the fairy fort, or the mound, is the dead man of the legend,' said Totey, 'what does it mean when it says, *but life allows?*'

'Yes, well I've given that a lot of thought, and I think

what it means is that the tunnel was an escape route. If the castle had been attacked, it would have allowed the occupants to get away with their lives. That would explain why Sir Timothy chose that particular hiding-place for half of his gold. He, no doubt, learned the secret from his father, and he too would have passed it on, but then as you probably know, his daughter's death had an unfortunate effect on his mind. He must have died without disclosing the presence of the tunnel to anyone, not even to his brother who took over the castle.'

'That still doesn't explain what happened to the treasure,' said Cowlick. 'We thought there would be a fortune.'

'Alas, so did I,' sighed Major Boucher. 'The only thing I can think of is that Sir Timothy must have drawn upon his secret reserve after all.'

'Then why should he leave one guinea in the box?' asked Doubter.

'Yes, why indeed?' said Mr. King. 'Unless, of course, someone else left it there ...'

'How do you mean?' asked Major Boucher.

'Well, we'll never know for certain, of course, but here's what I'd like to think happened ...' Mr. King paused for a moment to collect his thoughts and then continued, 'I'd like to think that ... that the young lovers *didn't* drown themselves in the Devil's Cup, but that perhaps they solved the riddle — after all, they did meet up around Wariff Hill, or so it's said — and that they eloped with the money that was rightfully theirs, leaving behind them a single spade guinea on purpose.'

'But why bother to leave just one?' asked Curly.

'Well,' said Mr. King, 'don't forget, that's what Sir Timothy gave them, or rather his daughter. A guinea, and a vague promise. Small consolation indeed, when he refused them permission to marry.

'So, by leaving one guinea in the treasure-chest, perhaps

they were letting him know, in the only language he understood, that love had found a way and had triumphed over greed. Yes, by jove, I think it's much more likely that it was the loss of the gold that drove Sir Timothy mad! What do you say to that, eh?'

Naturally, we hadn't thought of that possibility, and we found the idea of the young couple eloping with the treasure highly pleasing.

'But if you're right,' Major Boucher reminded him, 'that would mean the treasure is lost to us too ... and we need it far more than Sir Timothy ever did.'

'Maybe so,' said Mr. King, 'but I think there is treasure of a kind in the fact that the legend has been solved. Think of the marvellous tourist attraction it provides. I had doubts about throwing the castle open to the public before, but not now. Visitors will come to hear the story of the Legend of the Golden Key, now that we can tell it from beginning to end. They'll want to see the Devil's Cup and the secret doors and passages, and the place where the treasure-chest was found. We can display the chest, and the two guineas and the bracelet, and sell visitors' guide-books with the story of the legend. Yes indeed, thanks to you, my dear Major, and to all these lads, and of course to their dog, the castle is assured of a source of income from now on.'

'Then the legend will come true after all,' I said.

Mr. King smiled, and taking Felicity's hand in his said, 'But it has come true already — doubly so, I think. After all, the young lover found wealth, happiness and a bride-to-be, didn't he? And I too have found all three — for aren't happiness and a bride-to-be, wealth of a very special kind?'

Felicity and her father were delighted with that, and I don't mind telling you, after such high praise and fine talk, we were delighted with ourselves too.

Then it was time to go. My father said our mothers were

worried about us, and we had forgotten all about Old Daddy Armstrong.

Before we said good-bye on the front steps, Mr. King asked us how he might reward us for all we had done, and when we said we would like nothing better than to get riding lessons, Felicity thrilled us with the most charming smile you ever saw, and said she'd be happy to have us any time.

We were about to go when Cowlick gave me a nudge, and I reached up and whispered in Mr. King's ear. Cowlick and I had something special we wanted to try. Mr. King agreed, and you should have seen the look on everybody's face a short time later when the two of us waddled out wearing coats of armour!

However, armour isn't all the story-books make it out to be. It's very heavy, and I couldn't keep the visor on my helmet from clanging down. Everyone laughed, and we had another good laugh a minute later when Shouting Sam appeared on the avenue. He stopped and looked at us. I saw no more. My visor clanged shut again, I stepped into emptiness and clattered down the steps like an empty bin. I didn't see him, but I believe Shouting Sam turned and ran as fast as his long legs could carry him. Poor Sam, they said he was the spitting image of the running dead man himself. Come to think of it, he must have thought the same about us!

I gave Prince a call with my bourtree whistle and we took our leave, although not before Mr. King told my father and me that we could hunt in the estate any time we wanted. I suppose it was nice of him all right. Yet, I sort of wished he hadn't said it, just as I wished my father hadn't offered me that cigarette. For poaching's like smoking. Half the fun is in doing it because you're not allowed to do it. After that I gave up both.

ALSO BY TOM McCAUGHREN

The Peacemakers of Niemba
(The Richview Press, 1966).

From The Children's Press
The Legend of the Golden Key (1988; abridged edition 1983)
The Legend of the Phantom Highwayman (1983)
The Legend of the Corrib King (1984)
The Children of the Forge (1985)
The Silent Sea (1987)

From Anvil Books
Rainbows of the Moon (1989)
    Short-listed for Irish Book Awards 1990
    World English-language rights have been
    acquired by Canongate.
    French edition by Hachette Jeunesse;
    Flemish/Dutch edition by Facet Internationaal.

From Wolfhound Press
Run with the Wind (1983);
    RAI Children's Book Award (1985)
Run to Earth (1984)
Run Swift, Run Free (1986)
    Irish Book Award 1987
    International Youth Library choice
      for WHITE RAVENS 1988
    This trilogy also won the Irish Children's Book Trust
      Bisto Book of the Decade Award (1980-1990), and
      has been translated into a number of languages.
Run to the Ark (1991)